A Shade of Doubt

A Shade of Vampire, Book 12

Bella Forrest

Also by Bella Forrest:

A SHADE OF VAMPIRE SERIES:
A Shade of Vampire (Book 1)
A Shade of Blood (Book 2)
A Castle of Sand (Book 3)
A Shadow of Light (Book 4)
A Blaze of Sun (Book 5)
A Gate of Night (Book 6)
A Break of Day (Book 7)
A Shade of Novak (Book 8)
A Bond of Blood (Book 9)
A Spell of Time (Book 10)
A Chase of Prey (Book 11)

A SHADE OF KIEV TRILOGY:
A Shade of Kiev 1
A Shade of Kiev 2
A Shade of Kiev 3

BEAUTIFUL MONSTER DUOLOGY:
Beautiful Monster 1
Beautiful Monster 2

For an updated list of Bella's books,
please visit www.bellaforrest.net

Contents

Prologue: Corrine

Rose Novak was like my own daughter. Ibrahim and I had protected her during the first, most vulnerable weeks of her existence, and a bond had been forged between that child and me that nothing could ever break. Sofia and Derek knew that. That was why, when Rose and Micah had gone missing, they'd placed their faith in us to find them.

Despite their trust, Ibrahim and I left The Shade without any semblance of a plan. The first thing we did was hover around the island, scanning the waters closest to us, and then spiraling out further and further. About five miles out, we spotted an empty boat. Micah's fishing boat. Ibrahim and I landed on the deck.

"Corrine," Ibrahim called. He pointed to a splatter of dried blood at the bow. He bent closer and sniffed it. "Human blood."

Panic gripped me as I clutched my husband's shoulder. "Rose's?"

Ibrahim looked up at me grimly and shrugged.

"What happened? Where could they be?"

"Let's keep scanning the waters."

We covered a radius of several dozen miles more in this way, to no avail.

Either Micah and Rose had drowned and were now beneath the waters somewhere, or Micah had found another boat and they'd set off on it. But in the time that we'd spent, we should have caught them if they'd been in the water somewhere.

We returned to Micah's boat again. We looked around more carefully this time, looking for anything that could help us understand what had happened here.

I walked to the bow, eyeing the splatters of blood again, while Ibrahim looked around the stern.

"Corrine," he said. I tore my eyes away from the

blood and approached him.

"What?"

He turned to face me, a strand of black hair between his fingers. It was too short and curly to be Rose's, and Micah had blond hair.

"Where did you find it?"

Ibrahim pointed to the edge of the roof covering the wheel. It was at least six feet high off the floor.

"Whoever that hair belongs to is tall," I said.

"Of course, this boat belongs to The Shade. This hair could belong to some other resident."

"Could Micah have had an accomplice?"

"Who?" Ibrahim said. "We did a thorough head count. Who else on the island has curly dark hair and could have done this to Rose?"

I tried to rack my brain to think of someone. Truth be told, I couldn't think of a single vampire, human, wolf or witch with hair this dark, short and curly.

"Which means Micah could have been an imposter," I said, following Ibrahim's line of thought.

"I have a feeling that a black witch is behind this," Ibrahim said.

I shuddered at the thought. But why only take Rose

when he could have taken so much more? Why not take Anna? Why not use the opportunity to take over The Shade and overthrow Mona?

I couldn't make sense of the idea, but we didn't have time to stop and discuss theories. We just needed to find Rose.

"Where could they have taken her? Back to Caleb's or Stellan's island?"

"I doubt they would have taken her back there after the Novaks managed to break in before."

I stared out at the ocean, a feeling of hopelessness swelling in the pit of my stomach.

"I wonder what happened to the real Micah," I murmured, although I was sure I already knew the answer. I doubted he'd still be living if the black witches were indeed behind this.

Ibrahim sat down on the floor next to me, his back against the side of the boat as he continued staring at the hair, his brows furrowed.

We sat in silence for the next few minutes, both of us trying to think of what to do next but both failing.

Eventually the silence was getting on my nerves, so I stood up and reached down a hand for him to stand too. "Let's just keep moving… anywhere. I can't sit still like this. Let's just keep scouring the waters if we have to."

Ibrahim heaved a deep sigh, then stood up.

Both facing forward, we were about to vanish again when a loud thump sounded a few feet behind us. The boat shook.

We whirled around to see two blonde women—witches—standing before us.

"Brisalia?" Ibrahim gasped, staring at the older of the two.

I recognized them instantly. Brisalia and Csilla Adrius. Mother and daughter, belonging to the lineage of the Ageless.

Ibrahim and I backed up on the boat, exchanging nervous glances. These were witches we couldn't afford to mess with. Their powers more than rivaled our own.

"What are you—" Ibrahim began to say, but before he could finish his question, the two witches sprang forward, both leaping for our midriffs. I felt myself falling backward and braced myself to hit the water. But before we ever touched the ocean's surface, we vanished.

A ferocious wind engulfed me. I could barely catch a

breath before my feet met solid ground again and I found myself staring down into a hole in the ground. A starry abyss. A gate. Ibrahim stood next to me, the two witches either side of us. Thick trees surrounded us. We were in some kind of forest—where, I had no idea. As Ibrahim and I attempted to fight the hold they had on us, a force pushed us backward. We lost our footing and the abyss consumed us. As we were sucked downward, I caught a glimpse of the two witches leaping in after us.

I reached for Ibrahim's hand, gripping it tight as we traveled at furious speed. I gasped as the end of the tunnel finally came into view. Sunshine blinded me as I hurtled out and landed on a grassy lawn. Ibrahim made contact with the ground a few feet away from me. Scrambling to his feet, Ibrahim gripped my arm and pulled me up. We raced back toward the gate as soon as the two witches shot out from it. But as we attempted to leap back through, our bodies froze midair, an invisible power keeping us from falling through, resisting the suction pulling us downward.

We were sent hovering back toward the area we had landed first and dropped onto the grass. I cast my eyes around. A river flowed a few feet away from us, and a waterfall thundered about five hundred meters away. The river glistened with precious gems, the banks lined with trees. I could have recognized this river in my sleep. It was the river that surrounded the main city of The Sanctuary.

The Sanctuary.

I could barely believe that I was back here. Brisalia stood up, Csilla close behind her as they approached us.

"I'm sorry to do this to you, Ibrahim," she said, looking at my husband with genuine apology. "You were loyal to my sister for so many years, but we just can't have you meddling with things."

"What?" Ibrahim spat.

No matter how much Ibrahim and I tried to break out of the spell Brisalia had us under, we couldn't. She was of the line of the Ageless, and against her and her daughter's powers combined, we had no hope.

Once again our surroundings disappeared, and this time when my vision came back into focus, we were standing in a large bedroom. Its walls were made of stark white marble, as were the floors. It was oval, and there was a beautifully carved four-poster bed in the center. Light satin curtains covering the open balcony doors blew in the breeze. There was a scent of flowers.

"I'm sure you will find this place comfortable enough. It used to be yours, after all."

The two witches vanished before we could utter another word.

I stared at Ibrahim. He still looked in a state of shock as he looked around the room. We both hurried over to the open balcony and attempted to vanish ourselves once again. But as we tried to leave the balcony, we hit an invisible wall. We rushed back into the room and out through the main entrance, down a set of wide marble stairs and tried to exit out the door. While the front door opened, we couldn't walk further than the end of the porch.

Ibrahim and I assaulted the shield with curse after curse, but nothing we could do damaged it in the slightest.

Sweat forming on my brow, I wiped it with the back of my sleeve.

Ibrahim grabbed my hand and led me back into the house. As we stood in the center of the hall, we both looked at each other, panting.

"What the hell is this?" I blurted out. It had all

happened so fast, I had hardly caught up with the fact that it was real.

We were no longer on earth. We were back in The Sanctuary. The realm of the witches. My home. And Ibrahim's.

The last time I'd spent a brief spell here had been to escape The Shade when Kiev had burnt it down with the help of the other children of the Elders.

I swallowed hard as I looked around the entrance hall. It was uncanny. I still remembered living here with Ibrahim. When we first became lovers, all those years ago.

Ibrahim caught my hand and we made our way back upstairs toward the bedroom. We walked out onto the balcony. This house was perched on one of the tallest hills in the area and afforded a magnificent view of the heavenly city sprawling out beneath us.

This balcony… it brought back so many memories. It was the spot where I'd shared my first kiss with Ibrahim.

We were old flames, Ibrahim and I. We shared a history that went far back. Much further than the short period we'd spent together looking after baby Rose.

We'd been lovers before I first came to Earth from The Sanctuary.

He'd been the reason I left. I'd fallen in love with him. Hard. And I'd thought he'd shared the same feelings for me. But his parents had forbidden him from seeing me once they'd found out.

Ibrahim came from a family closely connected to the Ageless' line, the Adriuses themselves. Even my being a descendent of the great witch Cora wasn't enough for them.

Ibrahim's unwillingness to break free from his family's hold had sent me into a spiral of depression. My mother, who at the time had been the witch of The Shade, suggested I come to Earth. I'd wanted nothing to do with my own kind for a while. I'd integrated myself into human civilization and enrolled in a college to study psychology.

And then, when it was my turn to take my place as The Shade's witch, I'd tried to forget Ibrahim. I even performed several spells on myself to help block him from my memory.

I'd thought I'd done a good job. But when I'd seen him again, when the Ageless had taken my powers away and put him in charge of me, all those broken feelings had returned.

That period I'd spent with Ibrahim on Earth—when it was just the two of us looking after baby Rose—had been possibly the happiest weeks of my life.

He'd told me he'd regretted letting me go since the day I left, all those years ago. But I was afraid to get close to him. As much as my heart felt that it might burst with joy, I didn't want to have it broken again. I still hadn't been sure if what we had was temporary and whether he would return with the Ageless as soon as their business on Earth was done.

But then he'd refused to return with her. And the day of Vivienne's wedding, he'd asked me to be his, forever.

I snapped out of my bout of nostalgia as Ibrahim's thumb brushed against my cheek. I realized that he was brushing away a tear. From the hooded look in his eyes, I could tell that he too was remembering our story, standing on this balcony, where it all began.

I closed my eyes as his lips pressed against mine. When he lifted his head again, he was smiling slightly.

"I don't know what just happened, or why we're

here, or what will become of us, or Rose, or The Shade… but I love you, Corrine. And I never stopped loving you since the night we first kissed on this balcony."

More tears leaked down my cheeks. I knew that these emotions were the last thing I should be feeling right now. I hadn't returned to The Sanctuary for so long that all the memories it brought back of Ibrahim, the first and last love of my life, sent my head reeling. I sank down on the bed, trying to steady my breathing.

After a few moments, I managed it, clutching Ibrahim's arm. It was time we started figuring out some answers.

"I wonder where that gate was that we just came through. Whether it was near The Shade."

Ibrahim shrugged. "I have no idea. It's possible it wasn't even marked on Mona's map."

"Ibrahim. Corrine," a silky voice spoke from behind us.

A blonde woman had just entered the room. I shot to my feet.

"Thalia," Ibrahim and I said together.

She was Odelia's sister.

"Take me to Odelia," Ibrahim said, walking up to Thalia, his fists clenched.

A sadness filled Thalia's crystal-blue eyes. "Odelia is no more. Being the next oldest sister of the Adrius line, I am now the Ageless of the Sanctuary. In light of the many years you served my sister, I thought it was only right that I make a personal visit to answer any questions you might have, so you don't feel like prisoners."

My jaw dropped. "She's dead?" I gasped.

"She was murdered in her sleep."

Ibrahim's breath hitched. "By whom?"

"To this day we don't know for sure. But we suspect that it was a black witch behind this. It seems they are becoming powerful enough to penetrate our realm."

As much as we were shocked by the news, it was clear that neither of us were truly that sorry. Odelia had caused The Shade much trouble during her time, and to this day I hadn't forgiven her for taking my powers away from me—and for what she'd done to Sofia, leaving Rose and Ben motherless during the first weeks of their lives.

"Why have you brought us here? And why are you

restraining us like this?" Ibrahim demanded, glowering at her.

Thalia sighed. Drawing up a chair, she sat down and, gesturing to the bed, indicated that we do the same.

"I'm sorry if Brisalia didn't give you a satisfactory explanation. But she and Csilla had to hurry back to The Shade. They have some... preparatory work to do there."

"What?"

"Please, sit."

I was in no mood to sit down and I could see Ibrahim wasn't either, but we gave in to her request.

"The black witches must be stopped," she began. "If they are allowed to continue gaining strength, both the human realm and the realm of the witches—indeed, every realm—will feel their threat. They will not stop until they have made every species subordinate to them. Until they have reclaimed the so-called true glory of our Ancients. A glory that comes at the expense of all species other than themselves."

"What does any of this have to do with imprisoning us? We need to leave. Sofia and Derek are depending on us to—"

"Don't worry about the Novak girl," Thalia said calmly. "Hermia, my own sister, has gone after her. She's already located their trail and will bring them back here safely. So fear not."

It felt like every clarification only ended up confusing us further. "What? Why would—"

"The Novak twins—well, mainly the girl. It has occurred to the black witches that she will be of much use to them, far more than they initially thought."

"Why?"

Thalia folded her hands over her lap. "There is an Ancient still remaining. Lilith, her name is. She is one of the reasons they are gaining power so quickly. She guides and directs them. But she is ailing. One of the reasons they need so much human blood is for the rituals they carry out on her behalf, to keep her alive. She is hanging on to her decaying life by a thread. To deny death in such a way requires a constant effort, an immense amount of life force, the most potent of which comes from human blood. Since they know of the twins' unique blood, they want to see if it will help to prolong Lilith's life, if it will be more potent than regular human blood. Basically, they want to add Rose to their ingredients shelf. And also experiment with other ways she could be of value other than giving blood."

"What other ways could there possibly be?"

"I believe they see potential in her, to turn her into a witch. One of them. Perhaps they see her genetics as a strong foundation, if they train her right."

"What about Benjamin Novak?"

"Lilith consumes primarily female blood. Benjamin's blood is not of as much use to them in this regard. Besides, once they've taken over The Shade, they will get him anyway."

"Take over The Shade?"

"Oh, yes. That is still their plan. In fact, taking Rose will just make this easier for them. You see, what you need to understand about these witches is that they value vampire, human and wolf life alike. Humans, vamps and werewolves all have their places in their rituals. They can find uses for each of them. So, while they could have attacked The Shade full force, they would much rather gain their cooperation. They don't want to resort to mass killing in order to gain control. They see too many uses for The Shade's residents to just kill them whimsically and would rather work on coercion than brute force. Once they've done some experimenting with Rose Novak, and are sure they can use her, they will use her to gain cooperation from the Novaks. The Novaks will be much more amenable to negotiation if the black witches have their daughter, don't you think?"

My mouth dried out. I stared at Ibrahim. His eyes were narrowed on Thalia.

"Why didn't Odelia take the twins at birth if she knew what potential they had?" Ibrahim said. "She could have easily stolen them, just as she stole Sofia and sent her to Cruor. Then you would have run no risk of Rose falling into the wrong hands."

Thalia averted her eyes to the floor. "Odelia was a conundrum."

"What do you mean?" I asked.

"I mean she wasn't as rational in her thinking as most thought she was. There was a flicker of remorse in her for the trouble she caused the Novaks. She didn't want to take away the babies too, as much as Hermia and I tried to persuade her. She hoped that the witches would not find out about the twins. I told her that was a foolish move. Of course, it was only a matter of time."

"Are the black witches still interested in the immune, Anna?" Ibrahim asked.

"As I said, they will get everyone within The Shade. There's no need for them to exert themselves separately for her anymore. Rose is their key to Ben, the immune, and the rest of The Shade's livestock."

I paused, frowning. So many questions had been competing in our minds, we'd forgotten to ask the most obvious one.

"How the hell do you even know all this about the black witches?" I asked.

She gave us a knowing smile. Standing up, she touched our shoulders and the room vanished. We reappeared in the city's dungeon. I recognized this place. Though I'd rarely visited it, I remembered venturing down here once or twice when I was younger.

Thalia walked up to a cell a few feet away and pointed into it. Crouched in the corner was a ginger-haired man. His head lolling onto his chest, he appeared to be unconscious.

"We managed to steal one of their own. That's how we know all this. Meet Efren Hansard. Formerly a resident of The Sanctuary. Turned traitor many years ago to join the black witches. We caught him sneaking around the borders of our realm. Since he has not yet become a Channeler, he's not as powerful as Rhys and his family. I and several of our strongest witches were able to overpower him."

Ibrahim and I gripped the cells, staring through the bars at the man.

"The black witches will be angry once they find out what we've discovered. They will double their efforts to bring us down. But we had to do it. We had to know what we are facing. Now we are in need of actual cooperation with a Channeler if we are to have any hope of retaining our freedom..."

Knots formed in my stomach. I dared not mention Mona, in case they weren't aware that she was living among us in The Shade. But somehow, I suspected that they knew already. In fact, I suspected Mona was the reason Brisalia and her daughter had been hanging around The Shade. *Perhaps they are concocting a plan to steal Mona away from The Shade... thus leaving it utterly defenseless.* Despair clawed at my chest. I was grasping at any hope I could that they still weren't aware of Mona, since Thalia had not mentioned her yet.

Although there were still so many questions churning in my mind, I finally asked the one question that had haunted me ever since she'd first opened her mouth. "Why would you trust us with all this information?"

I feared I already knew the answer.

Thalia gave a soft smile. "Oh, I needn't worry about you telling anyone. Neither of you are going anywhere for a long time."

Chapter 1: Rose

Every second that Annora's hands remained wrapped around Caleb, it felt like they were wrapped around my neck. The worst thing was not being able to see Caleb's face. I had no idea whether he was returning her passion, her affection. But when he reached behind his back and unclasped her hands from him, stepping away from her, I found some hope that perhaps I hadn't lost him yet.

Still sitting half-submerged in water on the floor, I'd started to shiver from cold. But I felt numb to it. The shock of what that white witch Hermia had said about the black witches taking over The Shade, coupled with the shock of seeing Annora, had been enough to leave me numb to all pain. To make any bodily discomfort seem trivial.

As Caleb drew away from Annora, she tried to latch on to him. He placed her arms firmly at her sides. He cast a look at me. His face was ashen, more drained than I'd ever seen it. Then he looked away from me and straight ahead at the exit, focusing on neither of us.

"Those witches... We have no time to lose," he muttered as he rushed out of the room.

It cut me how his voice sounded so distant, so separate, when all I wanted was for him to hold me and tell me nothing had changed between us. That his feelings still remained the same. That he still wanted to return with me to The Shade. But he didn't.

Perhaps I am losing him.

Annora didn't even look at me as she followed him. Reaching up to a metal ledge, I pulled myself up out of the water. I was knocked to the floor again as the submarine plunged downward. My stomach flipped, and I felt dizzy. Instead of trying to stand again, I crawled toward the entrance. It led to a flight of stairs, and a dryer area that hadn't been exposed to the water Annora had let in whilst sucking us through the hatch.

I was surprised she hadn't orchestrated the rescue to keep me locked out and only suck Caleb through. Though Caleb was holding on to me. I supposed that was the only reason. I imagined she would have taken pleasure in seeing those two witches above water take me away while she escaped with Caleb.

Still shivering, I gripped the railing in case the submarine suddenly lurched again. I found myself in a passageway. There were several narrow doors on either side, leading to cabins, I assumed. I grimaced. They were all closed. I guessed that Annora had closed the door to the control cabin.

I was too drained to care just then. And too cold. I gripped the handle of the nearest door to me and was relieved when it opened into a small room with a clean-looking cot in one corner, a small cabinet, and a towel rack.

I rummaged through the closet and found a towel. Stripping out of my wet clothes, I dried myself. I found clean clothes in one of the drawers—pants and a shirt. They were both too large for me, but anything was better than remaining in my wet clothes.

Wrapping my hair up in the towel, I lay down on the cot and curled up in a ball.

Mom. Dad. Ben. Grandpa… I thought of everyone who was dear to me in The Shade. *Please, please be safe.* I prayed that the witch was lying. Caleb had seemed to suspect so. But it was the doubt, the not knowing, that was torturous.

I shut my eyes, trying to numb the pain and uncertainty boiling up within me. Scorching me alive. I should have been more concerned as to whether or not we had managed to get those two black witches off our tail. But my mind was too distracted by other worries.

After an hour or so, I heard the click of a door. I crept to my own door and opened it slightly to peer out. Annora had left the control room and was walking into another cabin, where she shut the door behind her.

I lay back down in bed, heaving a sigh.

I didn't know whether Caleb had asked her to leave, or if she had left of her own accord. Somehow, I doubted the latter.

CHAPTER 2: VIVIENNE

"Promise me, Vivienne, that you won't feel bad while you're away. I want you to enjoy yourself and not think about us. Can you promise me that?"

As Xavier and I entered the lobby of our hotel, my brother Derek's words rang through my head. I'd promised him that I would try, even if it proved to be the hardest thing in the world.

Given that we were trying to get away from the troubles of The Shade and the waters surrounding it, Xavier suggested we go somewhere far away from the Pacific Ocean. He'd suggested Santorini, Greece.

Neither of us had been there before, but we'd heard that it was a popular honeymoon destination. I wasn't picky about where we ended up. My husband was all I wanted. But now that we'd arrived in Santorini, I could certainly see how it had earned its reputation.

Xavier insisted we stay in the most expensive room of the hotel, the penthouse suite, right at the top of the pristine white building. The manager led us up there personally, along with two employees carrying our bags.

I drew a breath as we entered the suite. Although the interiors were spacious and beautiful, my eyes were drawn to the balcony. I took off my shoes and walked up to the glass doors, parting the blinds to allow the evening sun to enter the room. I opened the doors and walked outside onto the terracotta-floored veranda, warm beneath my bare feet.

There was a sprawling infinity pool to my left, a table for two with candles and a pretty flower arrangement in the center, and beyond, stretching out all around us, was a vision so eye-wateringly beautiful I could barely believe we were still on earth. The sea was the most brilliant blue I had ever seen. Perhaps only Derek's eyes could rival it. And the sky... there was not a single cloud in sight as the sun began its descent behind the horizon. I guessed that this place could even give The Sanctuary a run for its money.

"You both look like you have some tanning to do," the manager said, smiling as he eyed our pale skin.

Xavier and I exchanged glances and chuckled. The men left our bags by the queen-sized bed before they headed for the exit.

"I can think of more interesting things on our to-do list than tanning," Xavier whispered, as the door clicked shut.

My heart raced as he drew me to him and planted a long, tender kiss on my lips. "I agree."

Xavier cupped my face in his hands, heat sparking in his eyes. "You're blushing," he said, his voice husky.

"I am?"

He nodded. "Viv, you have no idea how beautiful you are when you blush."

I was sure that I blushed some more as his intense eyes bored into mine.

I reached for his shirt and began unbuttoning it while he unzipped my dress. He slid it off my shoulders, then reached behind my back and unclasped my bra.

He dropped both garments on the floor before removing his pants.

"I think a shower is in order," he said, catching my hand and leading me toward the bathroom. Turning on the monsoon shower, he backed me up against the cool tiled wall and trailed kisses along my shoulders.

We soaped each other down and when his hands lowered to the small of my back, I felt things were about to get a lot more heated. As he moved to taste my mouth again, I pressed a finger against his lips.

"Wait," I breathed.

I twined my fingers with his and led him out of the bathroom. We crossed the bedroom floor, leaving a trail of soapy water behind us, and stepped onto the balcony. Only half of the deep orange sun remained above the horizon now. I slid into the crystal clear pool, pulling in Xavier after me. Draping my arms over his shoulders, I pressed my mouth against his. I closed my eyes, relishing the feel of his tongue parting my lips. I wrapped my legs around his waist and pulled myself flush against him.

"Now," I whispered. "Remind me where we were."

CHAPTER 3: DEREK

To say that Ben's turning hadn't gone as I'd hoped would have been an understatement. As Sofia left the chamber, he continued convulsing and coughing blood—too much blood. He couldn't afford to lose this much. People had been known to die during this transition phase, when they were still vulnerable due to being partly human. As much as I could see he was in pain, I forced him to sit upright, hoping that it would stem the blood a little. No chance. If anything, he began coughing up more. He started to get a nose bleed. I ripped off a piece of the cloth he was lying on and tipped his head back, trying to at least stop the nose bleed. Again, it didn't seem to make the slightest bit of difference.

I'd never witnessed a turning with so much blood being expelled. He was looking paler by the moment.

The slab and the floor were covered in frightening amounts of blood. I cursed myself for not thinking to bring a witch in here with us in case we needed medical help for Ben.

I was about to leave Ben and go fetch Adelle or Patricia myself when, to my relief, Sofia barged into the room. She let out a gasp as her eyes fell on Ben, clasping a trembling hand over her mouth.

"Go find Adelle, Patricia, or Mona," I said. "Or any witch with medical knowledge. Whoever you can find fastest."

Although she looked like the last thing she wanted to do was leave him in this state, she sped out of the room.

Of course, there wasn't much even a witch could do at this stage of the process. Nature was taking its course. There was no way to stop my venom reacting with his body. We just had to hope that the transformation took hold of him before he lost too much blood to survive as a human. I supposed it was more for my own comfort that I wanted to know that a witch was there with us, even if there wasn't much more she could do than I could do myself.

Pushing him back down on the slab as he groaned, his body shaking and shivering, I opened his jaw and examined his teeth. I breathed out in relief to see that they were taking form.

Soon. Soon. I just had to hope that it would be soon enough.

Sofia appeared in the room a few minutes later, Adelle by her side. Adelle's eyes widened as she took in all the blood.

"His fangs are coming through now," I said. "Hopefully, it won't be much longer until he is predominantly vampire, and the blood loss won't matter as much."

I shuddered. *My son is going to be one hungry vampire when he comes to.*

We'd have to keep him as far away from humans as we could. It would be torture for him, trying to satisfy his newfound bloodlust on animal blood. It would be like trying to satisfy a burning itch by blowing on it.

But he would have no choice. He'd have to get used to it, just as we'd all had to.

"I suppose there's not much I can do now," Adelle concluded as she stood by the slab.

I nodded. Sofia hurried to my side, gripping Ben's head and brushing the hair away from his sweaty forehead as he continued to convulse and groan. She placed a kiss on his forehead.

"It's okay, Ben," she whispered, as though he could make out what she was saying in his agony. "It will be over soon."

I couldn't help but smile bitterly at her remark. *Oh, no. Once he's turned, it will have just begun.*

Neither of us exchanged a word for the next hour. We just stood, staring at Ben, willing his transformation to take hold faster. We all breathed easier once Ben's coughing finally began to subside, the blood he spewed out becoming less and less. When his convulsions became less violent, and his breathing had slowed to a normal pace, I deemed it safe to leave the Sanctuary.

I looked at Adelle. As I suspected, we hadn't found use for her magic. "Thank you for coming."

"It's no problem. I hope Ben will make a quick

recovery now. If there's anything I can do, just let me know."

As Adelle vanished, I picked Ben up and walked out of the chamber with him. Sofia followed alongside me, anxiously looking at our son's face. It looked a little calmer now, though it was still contorted with pain. His eyes were still glued shut. Even for me, carrying him wasn't as easy a task as it had once been. He was almost my height, and he was a muscular young man. He kept twitching every now and then, making it hard to maintain a solid grip on him.

We hurried back to our treehouse, and on entering, I headed straight for his room. Sofia stripped the sheets and blankets from his bed and covered it with towels. I placed him down and held him still while he finished the last of his convulsions. When I thought it safe to leave him, Sofia and I left the room and closed the door behind us.

We'd have to keep a close eye on him until he fully came to. Because once he did, he'd be ready to go on a rampage in search of human blood. We needed to have an ample supply of animal blood for him to guzzle down, or he'd likely go berserk. He might start tearing the walls down.

We headed to the kitchen. I bent over the sink, washing my hands, arms and face, clearing away the blood and sweat from my skin.

"Hopefully, the worst danger is over now," Sofia sighed, using the sink and washing her hands after I'd backed away from it.

I sank into a chair. She took a seat next to me. Even if I didn't feel confident about the state Ben would wake up in, it didn't mean I had to worry Sofia unduly about it. What would happen would happen, and we'd just have to deal with it. I reached across the table and clasped her hand.

"Derek, about Mona," she began.

"Oh." In my anxiety over my son, I had completely forgotten about Mona. "What happened?" I leaned forward, staring at Sofia intently. She bit her lip and looked up at me. Uncertainty and worry showed in her eyes. I squeezed her hand. "Tell me."

"Two witches from The Sanctuary, Brisalia and Csilla Adrius—sister and niece of the late Odelia Adrius—are here on this island as we speak."

There were so many things about that one short

statement that sent my mind reeling.

"What?" I spluttered. "How did they get in here? Why did Mona allow it? Odelia is dead? What do they want?"

She wet her lower lip, drawing in a sharp breath. "Odelia was murdered. I'm not sure exactly how it happened. Mona said they called her attention outside the island... They claim they want to form an alliance with us. I didn't have time to discuss any details with her, but—"

"I want them off this island."

"Derek... they said they can help us find Rose."

I stared at Sofia, unable to believe that she was even entertaining the idea of cooperating with them.

"I don't care what they say," I growled, scraping my chair back and standing up. I stalked to the door and looked back at Sofia. "Stay here and keep an eye on Ben. I'm going to tell Mona right now—"

She hurried over to me and gripped my arm, pulling me back. "Wait," she breathed, her eyes glistening with tears. "I had the same reaction as you when I first saw them. But Derek... how long has it been since Ibrahim and Corrine left? What if... what if something happened to them? They haven't made contact with us as they promised they would. So much time has passed, with Rose gone. I'm losing hope…" Her voice broke.

The way she was looking at me made me ache inside. I saw such sorrow in those beautiful eyes of hers. It cut me that there was nothing I could do to alleviate her suffering.

I held her waist and drew her closer to me, wiping her tears with my thumbs and kissing her cheeks.

I breathed out as she wrapped her arms around me, burying her head in my chest. I gripped the back of her head and rocked her gently from side to side.

Despite the burning in me to alleviate Sofia's suffering, I knew that desperation was clouding her judgment. I was sure that the witches were preying on us at this vulnerable time, knowing that we would be more likely to accept whatever they proposed out of desperation to get our daughter back. But that was insanity. We'd already suffered enough at their hands. I wasn't about to run even the slightest risk of suffering because of them again.

We couldn't approach them from a stance of weakness. From vulnerability. That much I had learnt about these creatures. We had to approach them from a position of strength. We had to be cool in our dealings with them, even if it killed us inside.

Although it pained me, I clutched Sofia's shoulders and separated myself from her. Looking her straight in the eye, I said, "We cannot allow these witches to run all over us again. We cannot agree to whatever proposal they have. I can guarantee you without even hearing it that we will be worse off for it. We are desperate to get our daughter back, but taking help from these witches will not make things better."

Tears began to stream silently down her cheeks.

"Sofia, we need them off this island," I continued.

I understood how Sofia saw these witches. She saw them as a flicker of hope, however faint it might be.

Me, I was a pessimist. I always saw darkness before I saw light. And in these witches' case, I struggled to see any redemptive quality in the manner in which they had approached us.

They wanted something from us. They had no interest in helping us and they would do all they could to wriggle out of any commitment they might make in regards to our daughter. We'd be risking the safety of our island by forming an alliance with them. I didn't know exactly what their motivation was, but I knew it wouldn't be for our benefit.

"What if they could actually help us find Rose?" Sofia croaked.

It was clear she wasn't going to give up on the idea easily. I led her to the sofa and pulled her back against my chest, stroking her hair as I wrapped an arm around her.

"I can't say for sure that they don't know where our daughter is. Perhaps they do. But forming an alliance with them is like forming an alliance with the devil. You know these witches as well as I do."

She gulped. "I do, and yet I can't help but feel I won't be able to live with myself if I don't at least try this. We know that not all witches are bad. After all, we are all still here because of witches. I just wonder, since the Ageless we knew has died, perhaps they have developed more humane qualities?"

I forced myself to consider her words even though my gut reaction was to reject them. The simple fact was, I wasn't willing to risk the safety of our people or our island.

I shook my head. "They are of the same blood as the Ageless. You said Odelia was her sister, for Christ's sake. They are one and the same. I'm as desperate to get Rose back as you are, but we simply cannot let desperation lead us."

Sofia paused, biting her lip. I hated to leave her this way. I was denying her this avenue while offering no alternative. But she wasn't thinking straight. I was in just as much pain as her over Rose's absence, but we had to find a way to get Rose back without these witches' help. We had many children on this island for whom we were responsible, not just Rose. We couldn't be reckless.

"I need to go to Mona," I said. "They never should have been allowed on this island to start with, and I don't want them here a moment longer."

Leaving Sofia, I strode back over to the door and left the apartment.

Chapter 4: Mona

There was a loud banging at the Sanctuary's front door. I doubted it would be Kiev. I'd just told him I wanted some time alone. Whoever it was, I assumed it must be important.

I opened the door to see Derek standing outside. His fists were clenched. I was surprised to see him so soon after Brisalia and Csilla had arrived on the island. What with Derek and Sofia's son turning, I'd thought they'd take at least a full day to come to a decision.

Just looking at Derek's face, I already sensed what their decision was.

"I want those two witches off this island immediately. There's no need for us to grant them a reception. They need to leave."

My mouth went dry as I stared at the vampire.

"A-All right."

"In future, don't let anyone from The Sanctuary onto this island. Ignore them."

I nodded, although I could barely focus on his words. He turned on his heel and walked away.

I clutched the door handle, guilt and anxiety welling in the pit of my stomach. Evidently, I was to be the one to tell them the news and then escort them off the island. I closed my eyes, trying to steady my breathing.

I didn't know why I was feeling like this. I'd thought I'd be relieved to learn they would be booted off the island. All I felt was anxiety as my mind whirred, trying to imagine how I was going to tell them. How I would word it.

Derek had made it clear that he didn't want me to wait around before removing them. And he was right. Yet every fiber of my being fought against it as I vanished myself from The Sanctuary and reappeared outside the wooden cabin I'd left the two witches in.

I took a deep breath as I clasped the door knob.

Just do it. Just get it over with.

I unlocked the door and stepped inside. I crossed the living room and headed to the bedroom. Both Brisalia and Csilla sat upright on the bed, looking unruffled as if they'd only been sitting there five minutes, showing no detectable signs of impatience. They stood up as both sets of blue eyes settled on me.

My voice caught in my throat as I tried to speak. I still didn't know how I was going to say this.

Brisalia smiled kindly. It killed me how wide her eyes were with expectation. Expectation that I was about to dash.

"Well, Mona? Have the king and queen granted us a meeting?"

I shook my head, averting my eyes to the floorboards. I gripped the sides of my dress, trying to keep my hands from trembling.

"You need to leave, Brisalia," I managed.

There was a silence. The most uncomfortable I ever remembered enduring.

Then Brisalia said, "I understand, Mona. That's okay."

I looked up and stared at her. I was surprised that she should be so easily accepting after the trouble they'd undergone to come here in the first place.

Brisalia was smiling softly. She caught her daughter's hand and began heading for the door.

"I suppose I shouldn't have expected much different," she said as she stopped with Csilla outside the front door. "Though I suppose I thought Sofia would give our offer a little more consideration, given that we could help get her daughter back. I suppose our kind really did put them through the wringer before. Perhaps their trust never can be restored."

I nodded faintly, then placed my hands on Brisalia's and Csilla's shoulders, vanishing us from the spot. We appeared again outside The Shade. We hovered over the waters outside the border of the island. I still couldn't bear to look them in the eye. I let go of them after I returned their powers and they hovered next to me.

"I… I'm sorry." My chest felt constricted, my throat tight. "I told you there were no guarantees… but I suppose I thought they'd at least give you a proper reception."

This time it was Csilla who comforted me. She

reached out and squeezed my shoulder, assuming the same understanding smile as her mother. "That's all right. I guess we weren't expecting a proper reception. Though it would have been nice."

I smiled awkwardly. Brisalia leaned toward me. Her perfume filled my nostrils as she drew me in for an embrace. As she pulled away, her lips pressed against my cheek. Csilla embraced me likewise. I felt my face grow hot.

It both thrilled and disgusted me that they should treat me so warmly. I felt like a monster for not telling them the truth.

That moment was the closest I'd ever come to finally admitting that it had been me who had killed Brisalia's sister, Odelia. But somehow, I couldn't. I just couldn't. Even though guilt clawed at my chest at allowing them to treat me like a friend when I'd done nothing but cause them harm, I didn't think I'd be able to handle the disappointment in their faces. Because the truth was, a part of me was a coward. I was still running away from the horrors of my past rather than facing them.

"Well, goodbye, I suppose," I said. I gave them both a faint smile and was about to vanish, but just before I did, Brisalia caught my hand and squeezed it.

"Wait, Mona. Before you go, there's something I want to give you."

She snapped her fingers in the air. She clenched her fists, then opened them to reveal a small box.

A gasp escaped my lips. My knees suddenly felt weak. I reached out and took the box from her. I ran my fingers around its gem-encrusted edges, relishing every contour of the small box in my hands. It had been my mother's jewelry box. My father had given it to her as a wedding present. Tears welled in my eyes as I tried to swallow back the childhood memories this box brought about, memories of my beautiful mother.

"You recognize it?" Csilla asked.

I bit my lip, nodding. "How could I not?"

Opening it up, I was yet again surprised to see the small oblong box was still filled with jewelry. It was my mother's jewelry, still intact.

I stared at Brisalia, a tear spilling from my eye. "How did you get this?"

She shrugged, still holding that calm smile.

"When your family passed on, my servant was put in charge of sifting through their belongings and keeping anything of value. I wasn't sure that I would ever see you again. I doubted it. But I knew that if I ever did meet you again, Mona, I would give you this."

I was speechless. It was all I could do to control my tears. I didn't know that I could manage to speak without my voice breaking.

"Thank you," I breathed.

"You're welcome... I suppose we ought to get going now. I fear we've already outstayed our welcome." She paused, reaching out and clutching my hands again. "We know that you've left Rhys and are no longer allied with him. I want you to know that if you ever need somewhere to go, or if you want to just visit home, you are always welcome in The Sanctuary."

Pain tore through my chest. I wanted to go more than anything, even if just to experience what it was like to feel welcome in my home, to live there without fearing for my life. But I couldn't. It would forever be a distant dream.

I nodded. "Thank you. But my home is here in The Shade now."

She withdrew her hand, her cool eyes still fixed on mine. "Of course..."

She looped her arm through Csilla's and, as she raised a hand to wave goodbye, both of them vanished from the spot.

I'd been clutching the jewelry box so hard, its gems were beginning to form dents in my skin.

I vanished myself back inside The Shade and appeared outside Kiev's and my home. I didn't bother to check if Kiev was back. Opening the front door, I rushed straight upstairs and locked myself in the bedroom. Sitting at my dressing table in front of the mirror, I stared at the pale, teary-eyed girl looking back at me. I reached out and positioned the box in front of the mirror. Staring at it, I traced it with my fingers once again, as though to memorize every part of it by touch alone. Fumbling for the latch, I flipped it open. An amber ring, two sets of ruby earrings, and a silver-plated amethyst necklace. Closing my eyes, breathing deeply, I could still remember my mother wearing them.

I picked up the pieces of jewelry one by one and tried them on, with shaking hands, in the mirror. I was about to replace them again for safekeeping when I remembered there was a second level to the box. If I recalled correctly, it had contained a stash of my mother's pearls. I gripped the small handle at the base of the box and tried to pull it open. But it was fastened tight. With age, I supposed. I'd lost count of how many human years had passed since I'd last seen my mother alive. I didn't want to force it open in case I damaged the box, so I closed the lid and replaced it on my dressing table.

I slumped back in my chair, my eyes still fixed on the box. The look of disappointment in Brisalia's face and the words she'd spoken before we'd parted replayed in my mind. And I felt suddenly disturbed.

As much as it wasn't fair, I couldn't help but feel resentment toward the king and queen of The Shade for dismissing my two old friends so unceremoniously.

Chapter 5: Csilla

Once Mona was safely out of view, my mother and I vanished ourselves to a cluster of rocks a few miles away from the boundary of The Shade.

I had to admit, I'd thought the king and queen would have at least granted us a meeting, considering what we'd said we could offer them. Their kicking us off the island so swiftly hadn't been expected, but we had of course planned for it. As we walked toward the center of the rocks, my mother didn't seem too fazed by it.

"You know, Csilla," she said, sitting down on a rock

and gathering the hem of her dress, "I think this actually might work to our advantage." Placing her hands on her lap, she licked her lips thoughtfully. "Yes, it would have been helpful if we'd been able to scope out the island for ourselves a bit more… but this way they are much less likely to suspect us. Out of sight, out of mind. We just need to trust in the preparations we made before arriving, and trust that things will go according to plan."

"I suppose," I said, sitting down opposite her. My mother cast her eyes about the rocks surrounding us. They fell on a small pool near her feet. She looked at me and nodded toward it. I stood up and walked over to her. We both leaned over it as she dipped her fingers into its center.

"Yes," she muttered, slipping herself off the rock and kneeling down over the pool. "This is deep enough…"

When she spread out her fingertips, a metallic liquid flowed from them. Heavier than water, it sank to the bottom of the pool and as she filled the pool with more and more, soon it had displaced the water. My mother stopped once it was filled to the top. She ran her fingertips over the surface of the pool and the surface hardened beneath her touch. As I peered over it, it took about three minutes for it to form a mirror. Both my mother and I stared at our reflections.

My mother smiled as she looked over her handiwork.

"Now, we wait," she said.

"How long do you think it will take?"

"It all depends on when he deems it safe."

I stepped away from the pool, manifesting myself something more comfortable to sit on rather than rocks—a reclining armchair. My mother did the same as she took a seat opposite me, and when it began to rain, she formed a gazebo over us along with an invisibility spell in case anybody noticed us there.

For hours we sat, watching the glassy substance, waiting for any sign of movement. As midnight approached, I began to wonder if something had gone wrong. I kept looking up at my mother. She remained calm throughout, no sign of the slightest bit of anxiety, so that calmed my own nerves. I knew if she suspected something had gone wrong, I would notice it in her countenance.

She was right to be calm, for as midnight struck, the pool finally stirred. What had previously been a reflection of ourselves was now a different vision coming into focus. Blackness at first, then a sliver of light forming around the lid of the jewelry box. As the lid opened further, a bedroom came into view. Mona and a male vampire lay together on a bed, wrapped in each other's arms, sleeping.

My mother's eyes gleamed as we crouched down closer to what was now our window into The Shade.

"Yes," she breathed. "Now, we see through Silas' eyes."

Chapter 6: Csilla

As our view left Mona's bedroom and glided down the stairs, toward the exit of the building, I couldn't shake the worry that Silas might mess up.

Yes, we had access to his vision the whole time, but we were powerless to ensure that he actually obeyed the plan we'd discussed with him earlier. If he decided to be disobedient, we'd have to watch weeks of planning go to waste. My mother seemed to sense my nervousness.

"Silas would be a fool to fail this task. This is his last assignment. After this, his bond to us is broken and he is a free spirit."

I breathed a little easier hearing this assurance from her. If she was not worried, I shouldn't be either.

She was right of course. Silas would be a fool. I sat back on my chair and tried to relax a little more as Silas began zooming along a beach. Two thick hands pressed against his eyelids, blurring our vision for a moment, to wipe away the rain that was bucketing down.

His speed soon found us entering a dense forest. Silas raised his head upward, scanning the treetops.

"Good," my mother muttered. "He remembers where to look first. We need not worry, Csilla. It's in his interest as much as ours to complete this task successfully."

I began to wonder how he wasn't bashing into things since his focus was on the treetops the whole time and he never seemed to be looking where he was going. Although ghouls like Silas were subtle beings—they could fold into impossibly small spaces and manifest themselves at will—when they did manifest, as Silas had now, they were flesh and bone. I supposed he had extrasensory abilities, since he didn't once smash into a tree. It helped that he was floating too—he didn't need to look at the ground.

"He's going too fast," I murmured. "He's going to miss—"

My mother looked up, throwing me a glare. "Calm yourself, girl, or your nerves will drive me insane. Have some faith in him. He will not do wrong by us."

I bit my lip, and averted my eyes back to the ghoul's vision.

My mother squeezed my knee as the ghoul stopped short suddenly at the foot of a tree. "See? Up there. Those are the Residences. He's spotted them now."

My stomach clenched as Silas rushed toward a tree and began zooming upward with breathtaking speed. I began to feel dizzy just witnessing it. When he arrived at the top, he cast his eyes about. He was on a wide veranda with flower pots and ivy growing up the sides of the walls of a magnificent treehouse. Silas scanned the building and then, on spotting an open window, he lurched toward it. Two pale hands with sharp black nails reached out and pried the window open wider before he floated inside it.

Now we found ourselves looking around a living area of sorts—comfortable seating and various types of human technology, which led through to an open kitchen area.

I wondered whose penthouse we had entered first. I was relieved that he'd found the Residences so effortlessly. I doubted by the size and lavishness of the penthouses that they could be anything but housing for the royalty of the island. Now, we just needed to find our targets.

Silas drifted quickly from room to room. I had to keep my eyes peeled. He moved so fast it felt like I might miss something if I blinked.

Finally, after what felt like the sixth room, Silas exited the corridor by drifting through another wooden door and this time we appeared in the largest bedroom we'd seen so far.

A dark-haired vampire lay in the center of the bed with a beautiful red-haired woman in his arms, sheets wrapped loosely around their bare bodies. They both slept soundly.

I wasn't sure what Silas was so interested in. I didn't know who this man and woman were. It looked like the woman was a witch, but I didn't recognize her. As for the vampire, I wasn't sure who he was. But neither of these people were our targets, so I didn't understand why Silas was bothering to linger so long in this room.

"Why doesn't he leave?" I whispered.

My mother leaned forward, watching intently, as I did. To my surprise, he reached out his gnarled hands and their solidity began to fade until they became almost invisible. His black nails made it easier to locate their shape as they lowered toward the man's head. I shivered as his ghostly hands sank right into the vampire's skull. The vampire didn't stir at all. Of course, he wouldn't feel a thing—perhaps a faint breeze, a chill around his head. For Silas' hands were now transparent, thin and light as air.

Silas was leaving his mark in this vampire's mind, and I didn't understand why. It seemed to me like he was wasting time tagging others when he should have been focusing on our targets.

My mother didn't answer for several moments as she stared, her lips parted, barely breathing. Then they formed a small, knowing smile. "Silas is just having some fun."

"What do you mean?"

My mother looked at me, now smiling more fully. "It's harmless. As long as he doesn't wait too long to reach our targets, we have nothing to worry about."

Two minutes later, Silas lifted his hands away from the vampire—still sleeping—and exited the room. We headed straight out of the apartment and rushed back down to the forest ground. Even though I was sitting solidly in my seat, my stomach lurched at the thought of traveling that fast down those enormous trees.

I was expecting him to immediately move onto the next treehouse, a few meters away, and continue his search. Instead he hurtled forward along the forest path, whipping through the trees, now in his subtle form again. I wanted to ask my mother what he was doing now, but she seemed to have had enough of my incessant questioning so I remained silent.

It was only once the trees disappeared and a clearing came into view that I couldn't hold in my gasp. I didn't need to have lived in The Shade to realize that he had strayed away from the vampires' residential quarters and entered the humans'.

"He's straying from his course already?" I couldn't believe my eyes. He'd only just exited the jewelry box and already he was straying from my mother's explicit orders.

My mother ignored me, her face serious as she focused all her attention on the window. Her face was expressionless—it was impossible to tell whether she was disturbed by Silas' conduct or approved of it.

Silas headed straight for the nearest townhouse. No windows were open, but none were needed. There was blackness suddenly as he seeped through the stone wall and emerged again on the inside of the building. A spacious hallway, decorated with soft carpets and paintings on the walls. A cozy home—and so typically human.

The stairs flew away beneath Silas as he ascended the staircase. Once again he drifted through a wall and appeared in another bedroom. A human couple slept in a bed. As Silas passed a long mirror fixed to a closet, he stopped and stared into it. I shivered. Even though I'd seen him before in the flesh, catching this unexpected glimpse of him in the darkness—his amber eyes glowing—made my heart hammer against my chest. His skeletal body was covered with thin, translucent skin that revealed the cold blue veins beneath it. He had jagged, shark-like teeth and tufts of long black hair hung from the base of his otherwise bald skull.

As he left the mirror and continued moving through the room, I wasn't sure I could stomach the scene I was about to witness. But, like watching a trainwreck, I found my eyes glued to the scene.

Gliding around the edge of the bed, he extended his hands toward the man and woman. They barely had a chance to open their eyes, much less scream, as the ghoul's black nails dug into their throats and punctured their arteries. As blood began to ooze from their necks, soaking the bedsheets, and Silas pulled away the sheets covering them, I could no longer look. I knew what was coming next.

Human flesh was a sweet delicacy ghouls didn't often have the opportunity to taste. My mother had often tasked me with feeding Silas back in The Sanctuary. He devoured all humans the same way—after tearing their throats out, he dug into their stomachs and ate their guts, swallowing the intestines whole, last. Instead of witnessing this nightmarish scene, I fixed my eyes on my mother who remained watching, still unflinching.

It seemed unlike my mother. I had seen how harsh she could be with Silas during training. She wouldn't let him stray even an inch from her instructions. To watch her so calmly witnessing Silas violating the very first rule we gave him was bewildering to me.

"Mother, what are you thinking? Didn't we feed him enough before we left? I thought the plan was to fill his stomach to last him at least a few days, so he wouldn't have to risk killing."

She didn't answer me for several more moments as she continued watching Silas' gruesome feast. Finally, she cleared her throat. "I'm not happy with the attention this is going to cause. If he was here with me now, I would punish him. But it seems he couldn't help himself. He knows once he has completed his task, he will be closer to freedom and there's no saying when he will taste human flesh again after that. As long as he's careful to hide his tracks, we have nothing to fear." She looked at me pointedly. "You can look now, he's finished his meal."

I looked down at the bed to see it soaked with blood, the corpses split open, fragments of their stomachs strewn about the bedroom.

Wrapping two strong arms around the corpses, he lifted them up over his shoulders and drifted out of the room. Since he carried these physical bodies with him, he had to open the door in order to exit. I winced, hoping nobody else was in the house who might notice. And then he was rushing back into the woods, as fast as the wind, gripping the bodies. He soon reached the beach and, hovering over a cluster of boulders, he shifted one aside and stuffed the corpses into a crack.

I was glad that at least he had the sense to dispose of the bodies rather than leave them on the bed. Neither my mother nor I knew how much experience Mona had with ghouls, or if she'd even encountered one before. We didn't know whether she'd be smart enough to detect a ghoul attack by examining a body. But we couldn't afford to take that risk. The moment she suspected a ghoul was present on the island, she would suspect us... and the box. Witches of The Sanctuary were known for the pacts they entered into with ghouls.

Silas had to keep himself hidden or our whole plan would come crashing down. On no account could anyone suspect that a ghoul was present on the island. I just hoped that Silas wouldn't slip up if he was to make feeding on humans a regular habit.

My mother seemed to sense my fear.

"We need not worry too much," she said. "All that

flesh he's just consumed will keep his stomach filled for at least two days…"

Chapter 7: Rose

I'd lost track of how much time had passed since Annora left the control room. But, despite the anxiety gnawing away at me, I could no longer ignore my hunger and thirst. It had been a long time since I'd last eaten, and I'd swallowed too much salt water when Caleb had kept ducking me underwater during our escape from Julisse and Arielle.

I got out of bed and walked to the door. Opening it, I looked out into the corridor. All seemed quiet. No voices. I wondered if Caleb had even left the control cabin, and where Annora was.

But my first priority was finding water and something to eat. I was beginning to feel a migraine coming on from dehydration. I walked from cabin to cabin, looking for some kind of kitchen area. There had to be a galley here. Annora had said that she had survived on this submarine for days already as she waited for Caleb to arrive.

Most doors were open already and I could peer in easily. I stopped short at the end of the corridor, just before the last cabin to my left. I heard the rustling of a plastic bag. My heart leapt as I wondered if it could be Caleb.

It wasn't.

I turned the corner to see Annora sitting atop a cupboard filled with dried snacks and a stash of water bottles.

Her eyes shot toward me, and I stood staring at her, speechless. There was a coldness in her gaze as she looked me over from head to foot, as though she was sizing me up.

She was sitting right on top of the food cabinet, her legs hanging down over the door. The only way I could gain access to the food would be by asking her.

I realized I'd rather put up with my migraine than ask any favor of her. Breaking eye contact, I turned around and headed back to my room, cursing beneath my breath. *I'll have to try again later when hopefully she will be gone…*

I looked back over my shoulder to be sure she wasn't looking after me. I almost walked right into Caleb. I stepped back in shock.

"Sorry," he murmured.

I remained where I was, blocking the narrow corridor, staring at him. I was expecting him to say something else. He didn't. His eyes remained on the floor, his expression stony as ever.

I stepped aside and was about to lock myself back in my cabin when he reached out and gripped my arm. He was still avoiding direct eye contact, but his eyes lowered to my cracked lips.

"You're dehydrated."

Not waiting for my response, he let go of me and walked in the direction of the kitchen. I remained where I was. As Caleb's footsteps approached the kitchen, I heard Annora murmuring something to him, though I couldn't make out what. Whatever it was, it was cut short as Caleb exited the kitchen and made his way back to me.

He was carrying a bottle of water and several packets of oatcakes. He placed them in my hands and stepped back. "If that's not enough, there's plenty more in the kitchen."

He kept his eyes on the floor as he continued walking down the corridor back to the control cabin. I stood staring after him as he closed the door.

I looked down at the food and water he'd just given me. At that moment, I felt I would have preferred him to just look me in the eyes. I would have given anything to know what was going through his head.

I wondered if he was perhaps still in shock about the whole thing. Maybe this was his way of dealing with it—to retreat into himself. I took comfort in the fact that he seemed to be avoiding Annora too, not just me.

Heaving a sigh, I retreated into my room and sat down on my bed. I ripped open the oatcakes and began chugging down the water. The cakes were bland, but filling. I finished all three packs and realized I was satisfied. I didn't need to make another trip to the kitchen for now.

As I was swallowing the last of the water, I almost choked as there was a rapping on my door. Discarding the water bottle, I leapt up and opened it. This was to be the second time in thirty minutes I was disappointed to see Annora's face instead of Caleb's.

She'd ignored me since I arrived on this submarine. As much as I hated her, I couldn't help but feel curious as to why she was knocking on my door. That was the only reason I didn't slam it shut in her face.

I raised a brow, staring at her icily.

She looked down at her feet and clasped her pale hands together.

"I thought we ought to talk," she said.

"About what?"

She looked toward the direction of the cabin Caleb was locked in. "May I come in?"

I was reluctant to let her into my personal space, but I did. I was sure to leave the door ajar in case I had to make a quick escape. I still didn't trust this girl one bit.

She walked over to the end of my room and leaned against the heater, still staring down at her feet. Finally she looked up at me. "Since we're stuck on this submarine together, we might as well be straight with each other. Firstly, I can't blame you or Caleb for striking up a… friendship."

Her choice of word prickled me. I walked over to her, looking her right in the eye, and stopped two feet away. I was almost as tall as her, and now that she seemed to be devoid of powers, there was nothing that intimidated me about this young woman.

"Firstly," I said, "I place the blame entirely on you for the broken man Caleb has become. Secondly, what Caleb and I share is more than friendship. The sooner you accept that, the better off we'll all be."

Her jaw tensed.

I was breathing heavily as I looked at her, my lower lip trembling with anger and frustration. I wanted to wring the neck of this little wench and throw her off the submarine so Caleb and I could continue with our story. Her expression told me that she felt no different about me.

She drew in a sharp breath, obviously attempting to reel in her temper as I was mine. When she spoke again, her voice was higher pitched.

"Pray tell then, what exactly do you and Caleb share?" She was attempting to maintain a civil tone with me, but each word she uttered was dripping with jealousy.

Her question made me stumble. *What do we share?* Though I'd not yet said it aloud to him, I knew that I loved Caleb. All his actions up until we met Annora had indicated that he felt strongly for me too. The way he'd risked his life to protect me. His agreement to return with me to The Shade even though I knew it made him uncomfortable.

But I was suddenly struggling to articulate to Annora exactly what it was. Love somehow felt too strong of a word, since Caleb hadn't yet professed it to me.

"We care deeply for one another," I said, wincing even as I said the words. It felt like such an understatement.

She crossed her arms over her chest, frowning at me. "Would you like to know what Caleb and I share?"

"I already know what you *shared.*"

She glared at me, then shoved her right hand in my face, brandishing the ring on her finger.

"His engagement ring still sits on my finger. I don't see one on yours."

"An old band of metal means little against actions," I

said, trying to keep my cool. "Back in the cave, he discarded you for me."

"I've changed, Rose. I'm no longer the person Caleb discarded. I've returned as the person Caleb swore undying love to... many, many years before he met you."

"If you had even an ounce of love for Caleb, you'd realize you've done enough damage already and stay out of his life." I narrowed my eyes on her. "You don't deserve him."

She looked like she was about to slap me. Taking a deep breath, she stepped back, trying to assume a calmer expression.

"Well, perhaps we should let Caleb decide for himself who deserves him." She extended a hand. "Let's just see who Caleb chooses now that I'm back, shall we?"

I gripped her hand, squeezing it in a firm shake.

I wasn't going to let Caleb fall back into this bitch's arms. Even if Caleb didn't love me I would rather he ended up with any other woman than this wench.

"Game on," I said through gritted teeth.

Chapter 8: Rose

Annora left my cabin and headed straight for the control cabin again. I watched with amusement as she knocked, only to be completely ignored by Caleb. Even when she called to him through the door, he didn't answer. Throwing a scowl back at me, she walked back to her own cabin and slammed the door shut behind her.

I was fed up of sitting in my own cabin, so while I didn't go to Caleb—I wasn't sure that he wanted to be around me either—I went for a walk around the submarine to stretch my legs. As I was descending a flight of stairs down to the storage chambers below, the vessel shuddered suddenly, making me lose balance and fall to the floor. My stomach turned as I felt us rising. I winced as my knee whacked against a sharp metal step.

What was that?

I heard two cabin doors click open. I retraced my steps back to the front of the sub to see Caleb standing in the corridor with Annora. He looked up at me as I approached, a grim expression on his face.

"We've run out of fuel," he said. "I thought we might be able to make it to land, but I miscalculated."

He brushed past Annora and me and walked toward the ladder leading up to the hatch. When we climbed up it, there was a grinding of metal. As the hatch opened, Caleb groaned as sunlight streamed down over him. I hurried over, breathing in deeply as fresh sea air filled the chamber. Annora was about a step behind me.

Caleb's feet disappeared through the hole. I hurried up the ladder after him, peeking through. We were in the middle of the ocean, the sun beating down on us. At first I couldn't make out any sign of land at all. But then I saw it—a faint outline of a shore in the distance.

I felt a sharp pain in my ankle. My eyes shot

downward to see Annora pinching me.

"Hurry up," she hissed.

Scowling, I took my time in climbing up on to the roof to make way for her. It pained me to see Caleb standing in the sun. He could barely see with the glare of the sun reflecting off the waves and bouncing into his eyes.

Annora brushed past me, almost making me lose balance and fall into the waves. I gripped hold of a pipe, pulling myself to the center of the boat. She walked up to Caleb, removing her shawl and covering his head and shoulders with it to shelter him from the sun.

"What now?" she asked.

Caleb stepped away from her and walked to the end of the vessel, staring out at the land in the distance.

"I didn't notice it on the map… but that seems to be an island a few miles away. We need to reach it."

He walked back toward the hatch, passing Annora and approaching me. He stopped, allowing me to climb back down before he entered in after me.

Shut the hatch on the bitch, I couldn't help but think as Caleb lowered himself down.

As Annora turned the wheel of the hatch shut, we all

stood together on the floor of the sub. "I'm going to see if there's any way to jumpstart the engine to move us forward, just until we reach the island. If we can do that, we'll be very, very lucky."

He disappeared down the steps. Annora, predictably, followed him. Unlike her, I had no interest in following Caleb around like a lost puppy. I walked to the control cabin and stared at the map. Caleb was right—this island appeared to be unmarked. I gripped the back of a chair as the submarine shuddered again, the engine beginning to hum and splutter.

A few moments later, Caleb and Annora entered the room. Caleb resumed his seat behind the controls.

"It restarted. We might just make it to land…"

I watched with bated breath as Caleb urged the vessel forward. It soon became apparent that we were nearing shallower water. The sea bed, covered in rocks, boulders and multicolored flora, was beginning to emerge beneath us. Eventually the submarine hit soft sand.

We climbed back out of the submarine again. Standing on the roof, I found myself gazing out at a pristine white sand beach lined with coconut trees. Further inland, there was dense vegetation. It looked like a jungle.

"What is this place?" Annora asked.

Caleb shrugged. We slid down into the water and made our way toward the dry sand. Caleb sped up ahead and rushed beneath the shade of the trees while Annora and I followed after him.

As I turned my back on the island and looked back out at the ocean, I breathed out deeply. *Great. Now we're stranded on a desert island.*

If Annora hadn't been with us, the idea of being stranded here with Caleb wouldn't have been so unappealing at all…

I quickened my pace to reach Caleb before Annora. She was panting already and we'd hardly traveled far at all. Apparently her powers had allowed her muscles to grow weak and lazy.

I sat down with Caleb on a fallen tree trunk, staring at her as she struggled toward us through the sand. I looked past her at the submarine moored on the beach. At least there was still a stock of food for Annora and me on the vessel if we ended up stranded here for days. As for Caleb, I had no idea what we'd feed him. If he refused to drink blood from either one of us, which I knew he would, he'd have to go hunting.

Annora collapsed as soon as she reached the shade, panting and spreading herself out on the sand.

Drama queen.

I looked out at the horizon. I didn't need a watch to see that it was evening. The bright orange sun was descending over the ocean. We had perhaps a few hours left of sunlight.

"The submarine must have a radio?" I said.

Caleb grimaced. "It's capable of contacting my or Stellan's island. Nowhere else."

"Damn it." I stood up, kicking sand beneath my feet as I paced up and down.

The truth was, I wasn't sure where we could head to even if the submarine was filled with limitless fuel. Even if the submarine hadn't broken down. The Shade of course was my first choice. But after what Hermia said, I didn't know if going there would be like riding right back into the jaws of the black witches.

My breath hitched. I suddenly remembered Micah. I'd been so wrapped up in the idea of losing my family, and Annora and Caleb, I'd totally forgotten that we'd left him behind. I turned to Caleb.

"What happened to Micah?"

He looked concerned as he shook his head. "I don't know. I lost sight of him in the waves as we were escaping Julisse and Arielle."

I wet my lower lip nervously. I hoped the witches hadn't gotten hold of Micah. Or perhaps he'd made his way back to The Shade… and whatever lay in wait for him there.

"You knew those two witches?" I asked.

"I knew of them."

Annora began to fidget in the sand, annoyed no doubt that she wasn't getting the attention she was seeking.

Caleb stood up, leaning an elbow against a low-hanging branch and squinting at our surroundings. "At least while we're here, it makes sense to sleep in the submarine."

I couldn't have agreed with Caleb more. I didn't fancy trying to sleep out here. God knew what kind of wild animals and insects came out on this deserted island at night. Even if we built some kind of shelter up in the trees, there could be poisonous snakes and dangerous insects.

At least the submarine offered some level of comfort in this situation. There were showers there too—basic amenities that I suspected we would begin to cherish in the days to come.

I shuddered as I realized we might not be any closer to escaping in a week than we were now. We had no communication device. Unless we found someone else on this island, we would be just as stuck here in a week's time. No closer to escaping.

We had to try not to think about the future and just focus on surviving.

Annora finally stood up and walked over to Caleb, taking his hand in hers. She stood right in front of him, trying to meet his eye. "I'm human now. You don't need to worry about blood. I can feed you mine."

I rolled my eyes as Caleb scoffed. "You honestly think I would sink my fangs into you again?"

She took a step back, looking hurt as he brushed her away.

"Once night falls," he said, "I'll explore this island while the two of you remain in the submarine. I'll scope out this place and figure out if it really is uninhabited or if there's perhaps a town or village somewhere with boats."

"In the meantime," I said, noting how red Caleb's eyes were becoming, "we should return to the cool of the sub."

Nobody had any objections, not even Annora, so we walked back across the sand toward the sub. Before we climbed onto the roof, Caleb gripped hold of the front railing of the vessel, digging his heels into the sand and pulling the entire vessel with his bare hands until it was fully inland. He lowered himself through the hatch and reappeared moments later. He leapt back down into the water and, holding the vessel's anchor, dug it into the sand. That would hopefully stop the submarine from getting swept away during the night.

Then he helped both Annora and me onto the roof, and we climbed back inside, sealing the hatch above us.

We headed to the control cabin where we all took a seat. Annora attempted to sit on Caleb's lap, but he caught her by the waist and sat her down in her own seat. I heaved a sigh, rolling my eyes again. I wanted nothing more at that moment than to have time alone with Caleb. To hold him in my arms, feel his lips against my skin. But it wasn't to be. Annoying Annora remained with us the whole time. Not many words were exchanged as we sat watching the waves becoming darker and darker.

Eventually Caleb deemed it dark enough for him to leave on his excursion.

I would have given anything to go with Caleb, to have some quality time with him, but I didn't want to slow him down. It was better he went alone. Besides, if I went, Annora would want to go as well. She wouldn't want me to ever be alone with Caleb.

It was with a despondent heart that I watched Caleb climb up the stairs toward the exit. Before he left, he looked down at me seriously. "Lock your door when you go to sleep." As an afterthought, he addressed Annora. "You too."

I nodded, watching him disappear and close the hatch behind him.

Annora and I stared at each other.

I had no reason to be out here now, so I left her and walked back to my cabin, locking myself inside.

As I flopped down on the bed, Annora's footsteps approached my door. To my surprise, they stopped outside.

"Good night," she called.

When I didn't respond, her footsteps continued along the corridor toward her own cabin.

I wasn't sure why she'd bothered to say that at the time, as I drifted off to sleep. But when I woke up a few hours later, coughing and spluttering as thick smoke choked my lungs and stung my eyes, I realized.

She was planning to make this a good night for herself. The night she got rid of me.

Chapter 9: Rose

A deafening explosion pierced my eardrums. I rolled out of bed, landing on all fours. I scrambled toward the door, reaching for the handle and pulling it open. A blast of heat scorched my face, stinging my eyes. A wall of flames engulfed the entire corridor to my left and had almost reached my door. I hurled myself out, flattening myself against the floor.

The flames were blocking the route to the exit. There was no way I would make it through there alive. The only direction I could head was right, toward the control room. Although I felt close to suffocating—my head faint—I forced my body forward with all the speed I could muster. I gripped the handle and pushed the door open before closing it behind me.

It felt like there was more oxygen in this room. The door to this room was thicker. I was able to stand. I looked around the room for any plan of the submarine, hoping I could find an emergency exit. I hadn't noticed one since I boarded. I cursed myself for not making myself aware of all the emergency exits as soon as I boarded. I was unable to find any plan of the vessel and the temperature in the control cabin was rising by the second. It wouldn't be long now until the flames began licking the door.

I stared at the large glass window and gasped. I had expected to see the moonlit beach. All I saw was a wall of dark water. The anchor had loosened—or been loosened—allowing the tide to claim the vessel.

I began scrambling around for a heavy object. I found a box of tools beneath one of the seats and pulled out a screwdriver. I didn't know if I would survive the sudden rush of tons of water spilling into this room, mixing with glass. It might cut me to shreds. But it was either this or certain death by burning alive.

I found a pair of goggles in one of the drawers. Donning them, I didn't hesitate a moment longer. Wielding the tool, I smashed it against the center of the screen.

It didn't smash. It barely even made a scratch. This was thick glass. I slammed against it again. A slightly stronger crack. Again and again I attacked the glass until finally it gave way.

I barely had time to hold my breath before water crashed over me, smashing me back against the door. The force of it was so overwhelming as the cabin filled up with water, I could barely move my limbs. The breath I'd taken hadn't been deep enough. As shards of glass ripped my skin, I was already feeling my lungs— weakened from the smoke—beginning to strain and only a few seconds had passed. The submarine began to creak and groan as water leaked through the door into the corridor, and the vessel began sinking.

Gripping hold of a pipe in the ceiling, I forced myself forward. Although my limbs were screaming in agony, I continued to reach for fixture after fixture until I reached the window.

I could only thank the heavens that I'd thought to

put the goggles on. I could see what I was doing at least. Without them, I doubted I would have had a chance in hell of surviving.

Squeezing myself through the cracked window, and grazing myself even more in the process, I kicked wildly toward the surface. A few more seconds, and I knew my lungs would give in. The weight of the submarine sinking was causing suction, dragging me down. I felt darkness closing in on my vision. Everything was becoming hazy.

I was about to lose all hope of ever reaching the surface when a strong arm wrapped around my waist, jerking me up to the surface. As I was lifted up above the waves, I gasped for breath too early and swallowed several mouthfuls of sea water. I choked and spluttered, gasping for breath. My vision was still unfocused. My head felt like it was splitting in two. Even though I had air now, I was finding it hard to breathe properly. Each time I tried, it was only shallow breaths, not enough to satisfy my sore lungs.

I was dragged through the water. I felt sand beneath me.

"Rose."

The goggles were torn from my head. Legs closed around my hips. Hands pumped my chest. Fingers pinched my nose. And then a cold mouth sealed over my lips, breathing life into me.

My vision came into focus for but a moment—enough to see Caleb's chocolate-brown eyes less than an inch away. Then I lost consciousness.

Chapter 10: Rose

A warm breeze blew over me. I opened my eyes. I was staring up at a roof of glistening leaves. In the distance, waves crashed against the shore. I tried to sit up, but hands pushed me back down.

"Don't sit up so fast."

I turned my head to the side to see Caleb sitting beside me. I was lying on a bed of leaves piled on top of sand.

His face was lined with worry as he looked at me. He reached out and touched my face, brushing hair away from my forehead.

"Oh, thank God." To my right, Annora knelt in the sand. She had a look of relief on her face. "We thought we might have lost you."

Memories of the burning submarine came flooding back.

"Would you like some coconut water?" she asked.

I just glared at her and turned the other way to face Caleb again. Caleb took the coconut from Annora and, sliding his arm around my back, helped me sit up and drink.

My head still felt dizzy, though my cuts seemed to have healed. I guessed Caleb had dripped his blood into my mouth while I'd been asleep.

He looked at Annora pointedly. "*Apparently*, something blew in the engine room and the force of the explosion unearthed the anchor."

Annora nodded. "I only just got out in time myself."

Clearly, Caleb had doubts about the story Annora had fed him. Though neither of us could prove that she had just attempted to murder me, I knew the truth.

But I wasn't going to bring it up with Caleb. I wanted to handle the bitch myself.

"So now what?" I said, rubbing my head. "We've just

lost the one safe place we had to sleep. Along with all the food and water we had there."

"I'd almost finished scanning the island when I heard the explosion and came running back." Caleb said. "I found nothing but jungle and beaches during that time. I'll need to complete the search still, but it doesn't look hopeful."

That's just great.

I shot another glare at Annora. I hadn't believed it possible to hate her more than I already did. Well, she'd just managed to prove me wrong. Thanks to her, we'd lost everything that would have made surviving on this island a bit more bearable—comfortable beds, showers, toilets, food, fresh water, and clothes.

Now we had nothing but the clothes on our back. Hell, I didn't even have shoes.

Images flitted through my head of Annora and I running around in bikinis made out of palm leaves. Caleb wearing a loincloth…

"What about you?" I looked at Caleb. "Aren't you craving blood?"

"I found a boar while I was out last night. How are you feeling?"

"Okay. I think I can stand now." Gripping the trunk of a tree nearby, I slowly propped myself up. Blood rushed through my head, blinding me suddenly. I closed my eyes, waiting for it to pass.

When I opened them again, I could see fine. My knees were a little shaky, but nothing that I wouldn't recover from soon enough.

I realized only now that my pants were so torn, my underwear had been showing all this time. I supposed I'd better start getting used to wearing fewer clothes…

Caleb rose with me, indicating that Annora do the same. "We should find somewhere to sleep tonight before it gets dark. We'll have to find somewhere up in the trees, near a stream. I passed by one last night, so I think I know where to look first."

I stared at the thick jungle lining the beach. Then I looked down at my bare feet. I looked at Annora's feet. She wore no shoes either.

"I'll have to carry you both," he said, following my train of thought. "We should leave now."

Annora approached him first, reaching her arms around his neck and wrapping her legs around his waist. It left me no choice but to climb onto Caleb's back. I made sure I bashed my legs against hers as roughly as I could as I climbed onto him.

Caleb was tall and sturdy—but both Annora and I were also fairly tall and with both our arms and legs wrapped round him, to say that there wasn't much breathing space would have been an understatement. I hated that I had to twine my limbs with hers just to hold on tight enough as Caleb launched forward into the jungle.

I just hoped he would hurry and get us there as soon as possible. Especially when Annora pressed her lips against his neck. I scowled at her and rested my chin on his left shoulder, where her smug face was out of view.

***

It was lucky for Caleb that the jungle was dense. The trees shielded him from most of the sun's rays.

As it turned out, what Caleb had seen the night before was more than a stream. It was a beautiful, crystal-clear lake. I breathed out in relief as it came into view through the trees. I was sweating. Both Annora's and my limbs had been rubbing against each other. As soon as Caleb stopped, I jumped off him and walked over to the bank.

Discarding any concern for modesty—Caleb had seen me bare already, and I didn't care what Annora saw—I stripped to my underwear and dove in. I realized as I was already underwater that I hadn't considered the possibility of dangerous creatures lurking in these waters. But at that moment, I couldn't think about that. It was just a relief to have fresh water. I scrubbed my scalp and ran my hands over my body, washing away all the sticky sea salt and sweat.

I wished I had some sort of soap. I caught sight of a bunch of exotic-looking flowers nearby. Hoping they weren't poisonous, I reached up and grabbed them. They smelled wonderfully fragrant. I crushed them up in my hands and rubbed them against my skin. They smelled better than any bodywash I'd ever used.

By the time I climbed out of the lake, I was smelling like a flower myself.

I caught sight of Annora bathing further along the bank. She hadn't bothered to even keep her underwear on.

I didn't bother putting on my ripped clothes again. They were dirty and damp and sweaty. I would have to make do in my underwear. Stepping gingerly over the rough jungle ground, trying to not cut myself, I looked around for Caleb. I couldn't see him anywhere in the clearing.

"Caleb?"

There was a snapping of a branch overhead. I looked up to see Caleb halfway up a tall tree.

"Up here," he grunted.

Gripping hold of one of the branches, I started to climb up myself. I tried not to look at all the gross insects I passed as I climbed gingerly higher and higher into the tree until I reached the spot where Caleb was standing. He was ripping branches and snapping them all to the same length with his bare hands, laying them out over thick branches to form a flat platform. I looked upward to see he'd already laid out two platforms higher up. He worked fast.

"There are three beds here," he said. "You will sleep on top. I will sleep in the middle. Annora will sleep down here, on the lowest level." He looked at me darkly. "Clearly, there needs to be separation between the two of you."

I kept climbing upward, past Caleb's platform until I

reached my own. It was surprisingly stable. Now I just had to figure out how to avoid getting eaten alive by mosquitoes while sleeping here in my bikini. Oh, and I'd have to hope I didn't roll too much in my sleep... Still, it was comforting to know that Caleb was directly beneath me.

I began tearing off leaves and laying them down over the wood to hopefully make it more comfortable. I didn't stop until the whole platform was covered in leaves.

I looked down at Caleb laying down the last slab of Annora's layer. I climbed down to his layer and began laying down leaves as I'd just done with mine. Then I lowered myself back down to Annora's level. *She can make her own stupid bed.*

Caleb leaned against a trunk as he finished, wiping the bark on his hands onto his pants.

Our eyes met for a moment before he looked away again, clearing his throat. The gentle chirping of birds surrounded us, the sigh of the wind in the trees. For once, I didn't have Annora's voice in my ears.

I didn't know if it would make him feel uncomfortable, but I didn't know how to stop myself. I reached out and held his hand, drawing myself closer to him.

I touched his chin, guiding him to look at me. The way he was still acting distant was killing me.

I just wanted to understand what was going through his mind, whether anything had changed between us, so I at least wouldn't continue thinking and acting under false pretenses. If something had changed, I would rather face the pain now than have the uncertainty drag out longer.

As my lips parted to speak, he reached up to my face, caressing my cheek with the backs of his fingers. His touch sent tingles down my spine. The way my body responded to him made me realize just how much I ached for his affection.

"Caleb," I said, my voice hoarse as I stared into his eyes. "I... I need to know—"

"Caleb."

I exhaled in frustration to hear branches creaking beneath us. A few seconds later, Annora hoisted herself up onto the platform. Caleb broke away from me, stepping back and eyeing her. To my horror, she was topless. She relied on her long thick hair for modesty.

Around her waist was a narrow wreath of leaves.

She might as well have chalked the word slut *onto her forehead while she was at it.*

"You will sleep here, Annora," Caleb said.

"Where will you sleep?"

Caleb nodded to the platform above us.

"And… Rose?"

"Still higher."

She looked like she was about to object, but, apparently having second thoughts, closed her mouth.

I wanted to scream. Unable to remain in her presence a moment longer, I grabbed a branch next to me and swung myself up onto it. I climbed higher and higher, hoping to block out her voice and distract myself from the frustration of being unable to get even two minutes alone with Caleb before she interrupted. I climbed until I reached the very top of the tree, and poked my head out from the canopy.

The view was both breathtaking and disconcerting. We were surrounded by crystal-blue ocean for as far as the eye could see. And the island was larger than I'd imagined. I could make out the coast to our east, nearest to us, but when I looked in other directions all I could see was more dense treetops. I lowered myself, looking downward.

Caleb and Annora were still standing together on her platform. It looked like they were having an argument, but I couldn't hear what they were saying. At least she didn't have her arms around him… or perhaps she'd just tried to fling herself at him and he'd rejected her, hence the argument.

Since I'd reached the top of the tree, I was about to begin making my way back down when I caught sight of a large bird's nest. I leaned closer to it and peered inside. It was empty except for a heap of dark olive-green muck.

I looked back down at my own platform, gauging the distance. Grabbing two thick leaves, I tipped the sloppy substance onto them and wrapped them up tightly. Once I reached my own platform again, I fixed the package to a branch nearby.

Something told me that it might come in handy tonight.

***

We spent the rest of the day looking for food. For Annora and me, we'd harvested several dozen mangoes, oranges and coconuts. The coconuts were particularly nourishing with their meaty flesh. As for water, if the water from the coconuts wasn't enough, we had to go down to the stream near our tree or the lake.

As for Caleb, he would just have to continue hunting animals each time he craved blood.

As evening approached, Annora and I still hadn't solved the problem of mosquitoes—being so close to the lake and away from the breeze of the ocean, I feared this would be a big problem.

We stood on the ground beneath where we'd set up camp. Caleb looked at Annora.

"You know more about plants than I do. There must be some here that can act as a repellant."

"Hm." Annora concentrated on scanning the area for the next half hour. I followed her around, paying close attention to which plants she pulled up so I could replicate it for myself if I had to.

Seemingly satisfied with the leaves she'd found, she crouched down on the floor and, picking up two large rocks, began to mush the plants and flowers together. She squeezed some of the juice onto her skin and sniffed it.

"This will do, I believe," she muttered.

She coated herself with the juice, then discarded the used plants. I picked them up after her and squeezed the rest onto myself, covering as much of my bare skin as I could. I ended up smelling bitter, but if it did the job, I didn't care.

Now that this task was done, we all climbed back up the tree and settled into our respective beds.

Caleb still needed to finish his exploration of the island, but it was clear he didn't want to leave me alone again, so for now he was putting it off. I hoped that he would ask me to accompany him the following day, without Annora.

As soon as I reached my bunk, I rolled onto my stomach and peeked over the edge. I had a clear view of both Annora's and Caleb's beds from this angle. *Perfect.*

I remained in this position for the next ten minutes or so, until what I'd been expecting happened. Annora slunk out of her bunk and began climbing up toward Caleb. Without wasting a second, I reached up and grabbed the green bundle I'd collected earlier.

I positioned myself back over the edge, waiting until just the right moment. The lighting wasn't great, but there were just enough shafts of moonlight trickling through the canopy of leaves for me to see what I was doing. I heard Annora whisper to him seductively, though I couldn't make out the words. Just her soft whisper followed by a moan. Brushing her hair away from her chest, she caught hold of Caleb's arms, trying to pull herself up.

And… fire.

Holding my breath, I tipped the bundle. There was a split second when I doubted that it would meet its mark. But, oh, it did. The green muck landed right on her head, oozing down her face and dripping onto her chest.

I quickly pulled myself back in case she looked up, fighting to stifle a laugh as she cried out in disgust. The beauty of it was her not knowing exactly what the substance was. Imagination was usually more horrifying than reality.

It could have just been an exceptionally large, constipated bird. But I hoped that she'd guess I'd dropped it.

Brushing away a few leaves, I peered through the cracks of my bed. She staggered back, still gasping. I watched as she began to climb down the tree—a late-night bath in the lake was in order, I supposed.

Nothing like a pile of crap to spoil the mood.

I rolled onto my back, staring up at the leaves blowing gently in the wind. I doubted she'd try anything else with Caleb tonight. Inhaling deeply, I supposed I ought to try to get some sleep. The plant potion I'd applied earlier seemed to be working. I hadn't noticed a single mosquito or other insect land on me since I'd been lying here.

Caleb let out a deep sigh beneath me. *What I wouldn't give to be lying in his arms right now...*

I turned onto my stomach again and peered down at him. I supposed I had at least a few minutes while Annora bathed before she returned and caused a distraction.

I slid off my bed and climbed down toward Caleb. He lay on his back, his arms behind his head, his eyes wide open. His eyes followed me as I crept toward him.

Unlike Annora, I didn't try to climb onto his bed. He sat up, staring at me and raising an eyebrow.

I was relieved when he broke the silence and said in a deep voice, "You were trying to ask me something earlier."

"Yes." I swallowed hard. "Caleb, I—"

I froze. A wave of screams pierced the night air.

Caleb jumped out of his bed and rushed down to the ground. I made to follow him, but he looked back up over his shoulder and hissed, "No. You stay where you are."

I moved about in the tree, swinging from branch to branch as I tried to get a better of view of what the hell was going on. I'd hoped at first that something awful had happened to Annora. But the screams were from more than one person. *How could that be?*

I climbed to the edge of the tree where I could get a clear view of the lake. I spotted Annora standing on the bank, clutching her chest and shivering. Caleb arrived by her side a second later, shaking her shoulders. Then he left her and sprinted away into the jungle.

I waited with bated breath for Caleb to return. I had no idea how long I'd have to wait. Annora returned in the meantime. Soaking wet, she climbed onto her bunk. I ignored her, keeping my eyes fixed on the spot where I'd seen Caleb disappear into the jungle.

My heart pounded in my chest. A second wave of

screams washed through the jungle. And then a third. A fourth.

The screams were loud, but they'd come from the distance somewhere.

I looked down at Annora. "Do you have any idea what that is?" I called.

She scowled at me and turned over on her side, her back facing me.

I kept waiting for a fifth wave of screams, but there wasn't one. They'd stopped. The quiet sounds of the jungle returned. I breathed out in relief as Caleb finally appeared at the foot of our tree and swung himself back up.

"What happened?"

He was panting. His hair was disheveled and his arms were covered with scratches.

"I have no idea. I ran to the source of the noise, or at least where I thought the source was. I couldn't see anyone. I even shouted out. Nobody replied."

I shuddered.

Perhaps we're not as alone as we thought.

CHAPTER 11: ROSE

Those screams still ringing in my ears, I was too scared to fall asleep. I drifted in and out of consciousness throughout the night, tossing and turning in my bunk.

As the early-morning hours approached, I rolled back onto my stomach and looked down. I was surprised to see Caleb's bed empty. Perhaps he couldn't sleep either and had decided to go for a walk. I looked past Caleb's platform toward Annora. Her eyes were closed, her mouth slightly open as her chest heaved gently.

I might as well do something useful with my time…

Considering Annora had tried to burn me alive, there

were still a few lessons I needed to teach her. Swinging my legs off my bed, I lowered myself onto the branch below as quietly as I could.

I scanned the branches surrounding me once again for anything that could assist me in my endeavor. There were a few more empty nests nearby that probably contained more muck, but she needed a worse surprise now. I was about to start climbing down the tree in hope of finding something in the jungle below when I was met with a sight that sent goosebumps running along my skin. A red spider the size of my hand swayed on a branch about four feet away from me. Its dewy web gave off an eerie glow in the moonlight.

Now I needed to figure out how to get it off the branch without it biting me. I leaned forward and reached out to see how easily broken the spider's branch was. It wasn't thick and wouldn't be hard to snap. I just had to make sure that the creature didn't go boomeranging to its death… or onto my face.

The closer I got to it, the more disgusted I was. I'd never seen such a vile spider. Its red body was covered with patches of brown fur, and its pincers looked long enough—perhaps even sharp enough—to be nail clippers.

As I was seconds from snapping off the branch, I stopped. Its bright red color led me to believe that it was poisonous. Although it was no time to start having moral quandaries, I couldn't help but think that my mother wouldn't have approved of this.

What if its venom is deadly? Do I really want to become a murderer?

The part of me that was closer to my father brushed the thought aside. *Eh. Maybe it's deadly, maybe it isn't...*

As soon as I snapped off the branch, the alarmed spider scrambled upward, its fat body quivering. I was relieved that it stopped where it did—a safe three feet away. Brandishing the branch in front of me, I made my way down toward Annora's bed. I prayed that she would remain sleeping soundly and wouldn't sense my presence. She must have been tired, because she didn't. Not even when I placed the branch between her legs.

I raced back up to my own bunk and, lying on my stomach, peeked over the edge. The spider was already beginning to make its way upward, onto Annora's leaf skirt. I held my breath as it crossed the leaves and began crawling over her stomach, across her bare chest, up toward her face. Her eyes didn't shoot open until it started climbing onto her face.

There was a muffled scream as she sat bolt upright. Her hands shot up to her face, which only squished the spider closer against her skin. Feeling its furry back, she lowered her hands again, now screaming so shrilly it hurt my eardrums.

She only had to endure the trauma for a minute or so before Caleb came swinging up the tree. Based on the terror in her voice, he'd probably thought one of us had just murdered the other. Gripping the spider's back, he yanked it off Annora and dropped it onto the canopy of leaves beneath them.

Spoilsport.

I moved my head out of view again. I found myself wondering if the spider had bitten her. She was still moaning, which gave me hope that it had. Now we just had to wait and see if its venom really was deadly...

Once Annora stopped sobbing after half an hour, I finally started to drift off. Then a cold hand touched my shoulder. I opened my eyes to see Caleb staring down at me.

"Caleb?" I said innocently.

"I want to finish my tour of the island," he whispered. "And I want you to come with me."

I looked down at Annora. She appeared to be sleeping again.

I didn't need a second invitation. I sat up and as he moved his body closer to my bunk, I wrapped my legs around his waist, my arms around his neck. He put one arm around my waist, supporting me as he leapt downward from branch to branch.

I held him tighter as we hit the ground and he began running forward. I closed my eyes, burying my face in his neck, wanting to lose myself in him. I wished he would keep running forever. Across the ocean, away from this island, away from Annora. To somewhere Caleb and I could be together without any interruptions. No distractions. Just us.

For now, I appreciated him taking me away from her, if only for an hour or so. I felt him stop running and he lowered me down. I looked around. We'd stopped at the other side of the crystal lake. I stared out at the beautiful, calm waters covered in lotuses.

Caleb caught my hand, pulling me to face him. He looked at me seriously. "You've been trying to say something for the last two days. There are no interruptions now. Talk to me."

Finally, I did. "I-I want to know what Annora's return means for us."

He remained silent for several moments, his eyes roaming my face. I was reassured that his grip on my hand didn't loosen after I'd asked the question. If anything it tightened.

I held my breath as his lips parted, fearing his answer.

"I loved Annora. Deeply. Madly. I doubt I would have put up with her all those years if I hadn't. When I saw her again on the submarine, as a human… and she kissed me the way I'd wished she would for the longest time, I was afraid. Afraid that all those feelings would return." He slid his hand beneath my chin, tilting my head up to look directly into his eyes. "But they didn't, Rose. I wondered at first whether it was just the shock of seeing her and the rush of feelings would come later. But they still haven't and now I doubt if they will ever return. She's… different than the girl I fell in love with. Even though she's human again, she just doesn't feel like that same girl. I've come to realize that I'm more in love with the memory of her than I am with her. I just feel… numb. You, on the other hand…"

I held my breath. He took a step closer to me, slipping his hands either side of my waist and resting them on the small of my back. Dipping his head, he rested his rough cheek against mine as he whispered: "My heart still races every time you glance my way, Rose."

The emotions coursing through me left me barely able to breathe, much less speak.

Catching my lips in his, he backed me up against a tree. I felt tears in my eyes as his lips caressed mine, slowly, tenderly. I relished every second that kiss lasted, and when he broke apart, I gripped his hair and pulled him down for more. I was starving for him. I felt like I could kiss his lips all day, just standing here lost in this perfect moment.

"So you'll still come back to The Shade with me?" I gasped.

He kissed me harder until I felt the tips of his fangs against my lower lip. "If we can find a way off this island."

"What about Annora?" I whispered.

He paused, furrowing his brows.

"Until we can find somewhere safe for her to stay, I am responsible for her." He stared at me, apparently reading my thoughts. "I can't just abandon her."

I feared he might say as much. Caleb was a man of valor and responsibility. After all, he'd grown up in a time very different to mine. Even after all Annora had done, I couldn't imagine him leaving a young woman alone and helpless. His old-fashioned values were a part of him that I loved, but in this case I couldn't deny that they were annoying.

"She's not going to be welcomed by anyone in The Shade," I said bluntly.

"Oh, I know."

"Then what could we possibly do with her?"

He looked out at the lake. "I don't know yet. But while we're figuring out how to get off this island, we have time to think about it." He turned back to me, pressing his lips against mine once more before picking me up again, guiding my legs to wrap around his waist. "We should finish scoping out the island now."

Even as he started running, I couldn't stop kissing every part of his skin that I could reach. I'd been scheming how to get back at Annora. But now I realized

I really didn't need to. Caleb had already chosen me. And that was enough to cut her deeper than anything I could possibly do to her. What Caleb had admitted to me was enough to wipe her out completely. I'd already won the battle. In fact, based on the way Caleb had just looked into my eyes, I suspected I'd won the battle before it had even begun.

CHAPTER 12: ROSE

Caleb ran so fast my surroundings blurred. But he evidently was taking in every detail as we zigzagged across the remaining part of the island that he hadn't yet explored. It looked much the same as the rest of the island: dense jungles and sandy white beaches. There was no sign of any human habitation here whatsoever.

As we arrived back at the spot on the beach where we'd first arrived in the submarine, Caleb stopped running.

"Well," he said, wiping sweat from his brow, "there's nothing here."

"Where to now?"

I feared he was going to say back to our camp, but instead he said, "I want to go back to the area where we heard those screams last night. Clearly, there's something about this island that we're missing."

I felt nervous as we raced back into the jungle and drew nearer and nearer to the spot.

He stopped, looking around a clearing covered by trees. "This is where the blood smells strongest still. It was around here that there were a group of humans."

"What's that?" I pointed to what appeared to be a piece of clothing a few feet away. He bent down and picked it up. It was a gray woolen shawl.

"You might as well keep it," he said, handing it to me.

I held it against my chest. This would be useful as a blanket, since it did get quite chilly up in the trees in the early morning and I couldn't afford to get sick.

Caleb stood and searched the area for more clues that could help us to piece together what we'd found, but he discovered nothing more. So I climbed back onto Caleb and we returned to camp.

I groaned internally as Caleb finally stopped again at

the foot of our tree, bracing myself to hear Annora's voice grating against my ears, asking Caleb where we'd been.

But as we climbed up the tree, Annora wasn't there. Caleb went to check near the lake, thinking she might have gone there for another bath, but he returned with a blank look on his face.

"She's not there either," he muttered.

Caleb did a broader search of the area, calling out her name, but with no reply.

As he climbed back up to me in our tree, he looked at me and shrugged. "I can't imagine where she's ventured off to alone…" He looked concerned. "I'll wait a few hours. I'm sure she'll be back. Wherever she's gone, she obviously doesn't want to be found."

I hoped to God that she'd just done us all a favor and drowned in the lake or gotten swallowed whole by a giant anaconda. *Or perhaps the spider venom has finally claimed her.*

But I couldn't shake the feeling that this was just an attention-seeking stunt. It wouldn't have surprised me if she was hiding somewhere, hoping to draw a reaction from Caleb.

Well, even if that is the case, I don't care anymore. Because Caleb is mine.

Chapter 13: Annora

As I'd floated in the lake, trying to wash out the green filth that was still plaguing the roots of my hair even after its sixth scrub, I'd sworn that I was done with this game. I wasn't going to mess around with this girl any longer.

It was time that I cut to the chase.

Then the next morning, when I woke up alone to find my nose swollen from the spider bite, and then climbed out of bed to spot them standing in each other's arms across the lake, I knew I couldn't wait another day to do it.

My first attempt at finishing her off had failed. It was just as well, I supposed. Caleb had seemed to suspect that it was me. This time I needed to be more careful. Because, once I was successful at getting rid of her, if Caleb blamed me for it, it would take longer to make him fully mine again. For him to forgive me. I'd hoped that Rose was just a distraction, to take his mind off me. Now I feared that she had come to mean more to him than that. The situation had to be handled delicately.

I was sure that, with time, Caleb would forget her and lose himself to me again. I just needed the chance to remind him who I was and why he'd fallen in love with me to start with.

But to do that, I had to eliminate Rose.

It might be true that I had lost Caleb's heart, but I would stop at nothing to reclaim it now.

The screams from the night before still playing in my ears, I left our tree and headed deeper into the jungle, toward where I thought the noise had emanated from. My progress through the trees was slow enough without shoes. I didn't want to waste time stopping to treat my nose.

The moment I'd heard those screams, I'd had a

sneaking suspicion what this island might be. And if my suspicions were correct, I was very, very lucky that we ended up on this island. Of all the places we could have washed ashore, this couldn't have been a more perfect arrangement.

It was afternoon by the time I finally got confirmation of my suspicion. Although my throat was parched, my feet bleeding, I felt a sense of euphoria I hadn't felt since first finding Caleb again in my heart that day I'd woken up as myself on Lilith's island.

As I stood in the midst of the jungle, staring into an old stone well, I couldn't keep the smile from my face as a plan formulated in my mind.

Yes… Yes. This will be a much more fitting ending for Rose than even handing her over to the black witches. They only want her blood, after all…

Chapter 14: Aiden

The moment Kyle and Anna discovered the bloodied bedsheets of their neighbors, Caroline and Thomas, the island was in an uproar. Kyle and Anna were both a bag of nerves as they came running to inform Derek and Sofia what had just happened. They'd been through such loss and trouble recently, and for this to happen just next door shook them both deeply. Kyle and Anna took Caroline and Thomas' two children—now orphans—into their home.

A large number of vampires and humans on the island were still convinced that the werewolves—in particular, Micah—were responsible for Rose's kidnapping. Many had held a grudge against the werewolves ever since.

Now, with the bloody mess that Caroline and Thomas had left behind, it was just another stab to an already gaping wound. All the doubt resurfaced again tenfold.

Derek and Sofia were forced to call a meeting in the Great Dome. The Shade's council, consisting of vampires, humans, and now werewolves alike—except for Eli, who for some reason had refused to attend—argued for hours. I remained silent throughout, listening to the arguments for and against a werewolf being responsible for this. The whole time, I kept looking at Sofia. I couldn't have felt more proud of and sorry for my daughter and son-in-law at the same time. Their daughter was missing, their son was still having a tough time recovering as a vampire, and now they had to deal with this new outrage that was threatening to overrun the island with animosity.

The entire time we were sitting there, we had to be aware primarily of Mona—we knew the werewolves were her family, and for that reason Derek and Sofia simply could not side with those opposed to the werewolves, even if they were responsible for this. The werewolves had to stay on the island, be they innocent or guilty. I saw it in my daughter's eyes as she struggled with this conundrum. She and Derek were supposed to be completely impartial, searching only for the truth for the protection of the humans on the island, yet at the same time they had to maintain a partiality toward the werewolves. Even if it was unjust.

No, the meeting was not intended to get to the truth. It was intended to reach balance and compromise, trying to appease opponents on both sides of the issue. Because if the culprit was found to be a werewolf, the situation would become even more tense. Neither Derek nor Sofia were used to ruling their kingdom this way, and yet now, dependent on Mona as we were, they had no choice. I could see Derek close to losing his temper on several occasions, and having to pause to reel himself in.

Back and forth the arguments went all day. By the time evening came and Derek adjourned the meeting until tomorrow, I was exhausted. I was relieved for Derek and Sofia. They had dark shadows under their eyes—far too dark even for vampires—and worry lined their faces. Now that the torturous meeting was over for the day, they had to return to more worries. Worries much closer to home.

I stayed behind in the Great Dome as the assembly piled out. Sofia and Derek remained seated at the table even as the last person exited. I approached them slowly, wary of interrupting their conversation. Sofia looked up at me and gave me a weak smile.

I bent down and kissed her forehead. "I don't think there's much I can do to relieve the pressure on you. But I just want you to know how proud I am of both of you."

She breathed out, rubbing her forehead. "Thanks, Dad," she said, her smile a little broader and warmer this time. She squeezed my hand.

"You both should get an early night."

They exchanged glances and nodded.

"We will," Sofia said.

We left the Dome together and made our way back to the Residences, where we parted ways.

I couldn't be bothered to wait for my elevator, and besides, I needed to stretch my limbs after such a long meeting, so with one giant leap, I plunged myself upward and, shooting up toward the canopy of leaves, landed on my veranda.

I headed straight for my front door, and didn't notice a shadow stirring to my left until it had fully emerged.

"Aiden."

I almost jumped with surprise to see Kailyn standing next to me.

"Oh, hi," I said, attempting a smile.

I hadn't seen her since I'd taught her and her sister how to use their washing machine.

Opening the door for her, I nodded inside. "Would you like to come in?"

She stepped inside and I followed after her. I gestured toward the couch and she sat down. She shifted in her seat, looking uncomfortable. Finally, she stared at me and asked, "Do you really suspect one of us?"

I heaved a sigh, leaning back in my chair, as I looked at her. The truth was, I didn't know. None of us had known these werewolves long enough to judge their character. From what I'd seen of them so far, they appeared to be civilized creatures. But I of all people knew that appearances could be deceiving.

I wasn't sure how to answer Kailyn without offending her. I shook my head. "I don't know," I said honestly.

Disappointment shrouded her eyes. "I know our pack, Aiden. Nobody would have done this. We may have a leaning toward human flesh, but we werewolves are loyal creatures. We would not have betrayed you in this way. Besides, many of us are grateful to be on this island and have basic amenities like running water. You don't know the life we lived before we came here..."

When I didn't respond, she shot to her feet and began to pace impatiently around the room.

"The Micah who took Rose wasn't Micah. I swear. My sister is practically best friends with the guy. He never would have done this."

I ran a hand through my hair. "I'm not sure what you want me to say."

Kailyn let out a soft growl as she walked up to my seat and towered over me. "Say that you trust us."

"I do trust you. But then I also trust our vampires. Of the two groups who could have carried out this attack, I'm inclined to believe that the werewolves are behind this. I've known the vampires on this island far too long to suspect them."

Her blue eyes bored into mine for several moments before she slumped back into her chair.

I felt guilty that I couldn't give her the straightforward answer she wanted. But I was being honest. "You shouldn't be too worried though," I said. "As long as we need Mona, you will always have a place on this island. We may just have to put some extra precautions in place... some strong boundaries to keep you wolves separate from the rest of us..."

Now it was Kailyn's turn to heave a sigh.

There was no point discussing this now. We'd been back and forth all day in the Dome trying to come up with a solution, a compromise, that would keep all parties satisfied. I was sick of this topic now. I stood up and walked over to the kitchen. Since she was still in her human form, I figured I should offer her a refreshment.

"Do you want something to drink?"

"What do you have?"

I opened my cupboard and scanned the shelves. I smiled bitterly at the homemade chamomile tea bags that Adelle used to love when she visited me. I hadn't touched the chamomile since I'd last seen her, and I guessed that it would be a while before I could bear to make it again.

"How does herbal tea sound? Elderberry, nettle, mint…"

"I'll try elderberry."

I set about preparing the tea. Kailyn walked over to me as I did. Leaning against the kitchen counter as the kettle boiled, she cast her eyes around my apartment.

"So you live in this big place all by yourself, huh?" She threw me a sideways glance.

"Yes."

A silence fell between us as I busied myself preparing the tea. I set a cup down for her and we sat opposite each other. I watched her sip it cautiously. She reached for the honey in the center of the table and added a dollop. Her freckled face lit up as she tasted the drink.

She looked up, and our eyes met. Her expression was serious.

"You know, I lost my partner too."

"Oh," I said, taken aback. "I… I'm sorry to hear that."

She breathed in deeply, and a flicker of pain crossed her face. This was hardly turning out to be the light-hearted conversation I'd hoped to lead us toward, but somehow I was touched that she would choose to share something like this with me.

"My mate," she continued, tracing the rim of her cup with her index finger as she stared down at her tea, "he was killed back in the supernatural realm. During an attack by ogres—relatives of Brett's, actually. My mate was the one leading everyone to charge. He went first. Got speared through the heart."

I guessed that this must have happened long ago, because she spoke calmly, as though she was just reflecting on a memory. Though her jaw still clenched. It reminded me of how I thought of Camilla now... as a distant memory. Except for when my daughter spoke of her—somehow that always sliced open the wounds afresh and it took a while to stem the bleeding.

I reached for Kailyn's hand across the table and squeezed it. She locked eyes with me and smiled.

"Don't worry," she said. "I won't break down on you. This happened many years ago."

I was about to respond when there was a rapping at

the door. I couldn't imagine who it might be. I doubted it would be Derek or Sofia—they had both looked ready to flop into bed after the exhaustion of the day.

I peered through the spy hole and swung open the door. I found myself face to face with Eli. His expression was serious, his eyes intense as he looked at me.

"Eli? What brings you here?"

"May I come in?"

"Of course," I stepped aside to allow him entrance. His eyes fell on Kailyn sitting at the table before he turned round to look at me.

His brows were furrowed, his face agitated. I had no idea what could have caused such disturbance in him. He normally avoided conflict at all costs.

"How come you weren't at the meeting today? Are you all right?"

Eli scoffed, then began pacing up and down the room.

I exchanged glances with Kailyn. She looked just as confused as I felt. When he still failed to respond to me, I reached out and gripped his shoulder.

"Eli, what's—?"

His hand shot out, knocking my hand away from him. "Don't touch me," he snarled.

I was so stunned by his behavior, I staggered back, barely believing what I was seeing.

His breathing became louder and more uneven by the second. He took a step closer to me, and finally spoke what was on his mind. "I saw you with Adelle down by the lake last night."

His words knocked the breath right out of me. My face contorted with confusion. "What?"

"Don't mess with me, Aiden," he snapped, his face now merely inches from my own.

My shock was beginning to turn into anger at his accusatory tone of voice. "I wasn't even at the lake last night," I said. "And Adelle and I are just friends. Even if I did feel something for her, I would never, and I mean never, poach another man's woman."

My words barely seemed to register. "How long have you two been seeing each other?" His hands shot out and gripped the collar of my shirt.

I clutched his hands, pushing them away from me.

What is wrong with this man? He's crazed.

My motion only seemed to agitate him further. His

hands shot out again, this time, to my shock, his claws extending. I had to jump back to avoid being grazed.

I stared at him, stunned. "Eli," I gasped. "What the hell?"

He lurched forward, aiming for me again. I caught both his forearms before he could reach me and pushed him backward.

By now, Kailyn had abandoned her tea, too shocked by what was going on. She approached Eli from behind and attempted to restrain him. But as soon as she was within three feet of him, he lashed out at her too, catching her cheek with the tip of his claw.

Sweat dripped from his forehead, his chest heaving. "You're a cheat, Aiden," he hissed.

That hit a raw nerve.

"How dare you," I growled. "Whomever you saw Adelle with last night, it was not me."

I didn't wait for Eli to lunge again. I dove for his waist, sending us both thudding to the floor. Gripping his neck with one hand, placing my other round his back, I flipped him over until he was lying face down on the floor.

Perhaps the one advantage I had over him was that,

despite being a vampire, Eli was not trained in combat. He used his brain far more than he ever used his muscles. So he barely had time to struggle as I snapped his neck with one swift motion.

There was a grunt in the corner. I turned to see that Kailyn had now turned into a werewolf. She padded over to me, and we both stared down at Eli's unconscious form.

He'd be back to normal soon enough. I grimaced, thinking that we'd have to take him to Adelle to get fixed up and I'd have to speak to her.

I didn't know what to think as I stared down at Eli— always the most gentle of people. It sent chills down my spine, the way he had looked at me with such hatred... such darkness. How he could doubt me, and what I had done to deserve such doubt, I could only wonder.

And who had he seen down by the lake last night? How had he managed to mistake that man for me?

I could only wonder what had gotten into his head.

CHAPTER 15: SOFIA

During the second day's meeting at the Great Dome, we finally came to a decision—albeit temporary. Mona would enforce a boundary, separating their part of the island from ours. No werewolf could cross it without permission.

We'd discussed the idea the day before, but I'd felt deeply uncomfortable about it. Now, after another day of discussion, we were no further forward. It seemed that this was our only choice if we wanted to keep this island from going under.

I hated it. It caused a divide far deeper than the

physical. I had begun to make friends with them. It felt like we were going backwards. I was grateful at least that Mona seemed to be understanding about it. Although she'd made clear in no uncertain terms that the werewolves were like her family, she was at least helping us deal with the situation and come to a compromise.

Once this was decided upon, Derek and I paid a visit to Kyle and Anna, who were doing their best to care for Caroline and Thomas' children—a ten-year-old boy and a thirteen-year-old girl. Jack and Stephanie.

Our witches were still scouring the island. I hoped they'd find the bodies soon and we would be closer to discovering the cause of their deaths. Part of me was afraid to find out who would have done this. If it was a vampire, it would be devastating—likewise, if it was indeed a werewolf, the animosity would become greater and there would be no chance of getting the boundary removed any time soon.

But if it was not a vampire or a werewolf, the other explanation was far more chilling. I wondered if we could have another imposter living among us, just as we'd had Micah.

After the meeting was over, I called Mona to stay

behind with Derek and me. From the look on her face, she seemed to guess what this was about.

"We need to screen everyone on this island. Just in case an imposter has managed to infiltrate us," she said, before we could even express ourselves.

Derek and I nodded.

"As soon as possible," Derek said.

"How will we do it?" I asked.

Mona took a seat next to us, placing a palm over her forehead.

"We'll have to arrange for every single inhabitant of this island to see me. I'll cast a spell on each that will force them to reveal their true forms."

I breathed out, just thinking about what a colossal job this would be.

Derek stood up and began making his way to the exit of the Great Dome. "We have no time to lose," he called back. "I'm going to start appointing managers to help with this."

I realized with a shudder that we'd even have to screen the children. Of course, I wasn't sure why a black witch would bother to kill Caroline and Thomas. But we ought to screen them anyway. In fact, we should have done this the moment we suspected Micah had been an imposter.

I exchanged a few more words with Mona before we parted ways. I needed to return to our penthouse to check on Ben.

As I neared our treehouse, I heard arguing booming down from the trees above. It was coming from Ashley and Landis' penthouse.

Not wanting to eavesdrop, I placed my hands over my ears and hurried away, but the tone of their voices shook me. I'd never heard them shout like that at each other.

Everyone is just feeling this stress. Just as Eli had snapped so easily with my father at a simple misunderstanding. It was a surprise to all of us that Adelle would be cheating with another man, but I knew that man wouldn't be my father. I fully believed my father when he said he would never do something like that.

I hurried up to our penthouse and pushed open the door. It was so hard leaving Ben at home while Derek and I attended to the affairs of the island. My stomach was in knots because, even after all this time since his turning, Ben still hadn't come to. Jason and Ariana had recovered much faster.

I went straight to Ben's bedroom and, unlocking the door, peered inside.

I gasped to see my son sitting bolt upright in the gloom. He was sitting on the edge of his bed, his eyes fixed on the mirror. He didn't even register my entrance. When I recovered from the shock, relief rushed through me. He had finally come to.

"Ben," I said, hurrying over to him.

His eyes remained fixed on the mirror. It was the first time I'd seen them open fully. My breath hitched. Now, as a vampire, Ben looked so much like Derek it was uncanny. His green eyes were just as intense as Derek's blue ones.

I touched his arm and shook him a little. "Ben?" Still he ignored me. "Ben, are you okay?"

He seemed to be in a daze, and yet his eyes were not glassy. They were quite focused, staring at his reflection in the mirror.

I stood in front of the mirror, blocking his view of it, and forced his head to face me.

"How are you feeling?"

He raised his eyes to me slowly, his jaw tensing. When he spoke finally, it was through harsh, uneven breathing. "I… need… blood."

I caught his hand and pulled him up out of his bedroom, leading him to the kitchen. The coldness of his hand sent guilt running through me. I could only imagine the guilt Derek would feel on seeing him finally, recovered and fully transformed.

I pulled out a jug of blood from the fridge and poured him a glass. He stared at it on the table. He raised the glass and took a sip, then dropped it, doubling over and coughing. It was disgusting, and it would be torture for Ben having to drink this when all he craved was fresh, hot human blood. But he had to get used to it.

"I can't drink this," he gasped.

He staggered back, away from the kitchen, wiping his mouth on his sleeve. Then he moved toward the front door. My heartbeat quickening, I rushed toward him. But it was too late. In barely the blink of an eye, he'd ripped open the door and leapt off the veranda.

Chapter 16: Ben

I landed in a tree opposite our own and leapt from branch to branch until I'd made it back down to the ground.

My brain was in a fog. I didn't know what I was doing or why I was doing it. All I knew was that I needed to get away from the stench of the blood my mother had just passed to me. It made my stomach turn. I heard my mother's shouts, and the sound of her running after me, but I ran forward with speed I'd thought impossible even for a vampire.

I caught the scent of hot blood in the air, coming

from the Vale, and my stomach clenched. Although every fiber of my being was aching to run in that direction, I couldn't allow myself to—at least I had that much presence of mind.

I kept running until I reached the ocean. And I didn't stop. I dove in, burying my head beneath the waves as if the cool waters would help to extinguish the furnace in my stomach.

"Ben!" A female called my name as I ducked once again beneath the waves. It wasn't my mother this time. I looked up to see Abby. She was already wading through the waters toward me. I kicked back and swam away from her.

She was in no danger from me, but somehow I didn't want anyone approaching me for miles. I just wanted complete space. Everything about The Shade suddenly seemed closed, claustrophobic.

I swam further and further down the beach until Abby gave up on following me. Even though she was a vampire herself, her speed was no match for mine. I looked back to see her silhouette bobbing in the water in the distance.

Every part of me felt on fire. I didn't even know who

I was any more. The bloodlust was consuming all rational thought. One vision replayed over and over in my mind—ripping open a human's throat and drinking until they had no breath left to spend. Until their fragile bodies collapsed in my arms. I could barely even concentrate on my surroundings, I was so consumed with the vision.

I was afraid that the first time I laid eyes on a human, I wouldn't be able to stop myself from ripping their throat out. It was horrifying to realize that the vision both disgusted and delighted me.

I continued swimming, for how long, I wasn't sure. I noticed my mother following me along the beach, keeping watch on me. I was glad that she didn't follow me in. That she gave me this space.

Although I felt close to passing out from hunger, I forced myself to remain in the water. I was afraid of what might happen if I allowed myself back on land.

"Ben!" This time it was the baritone voice of my father.

I'd been expecting him to arrive at some point.

Unlike my mother, he immediately leapt into the water. It seemed that he was the only one who could match my speed. He caught up with me and, gripping my arm, pulled me round to face him. "Ben," he repeated, staring at me with a mixture of concern and horror. His grip around my arm tightened. "You need to drink the blood your mother gave you."

I growled and pulled away from his grasp, swimming further up the shore. My father caught up with me again, gripping me firmer this time and pulling me toward the shore. I thrashed against him, but he kept holding me and wrestled me into submission. By the time we reached the shore, I was still fighting against him.

He pinned me down against the sand, my arms locked in an arm bar behind me as he forced me to stand up.

"If you don't fill yourself with animal blood, you won't be able to keep yourself from attacking humans."

I stopped struggling against my father as a moment of clarity fell upon me.

So this is what it's like to be a vampire.

At that moment, I didn't understand why I'd ever wanted to become one. Had I known this was what it would feel like, I doubted I ever would have wanted to turn. Of course, my parents had described what it was like. But no words could have prepared me for the pain burning through me now.

Still gripping my arm tightly, my father ran with me until we reached my mother and Abby, waiting for us on the shore. I allowed my father to lead me back to the penthouse. My chest heaved as I stared at the animal blood still waiting for me on the table.

My hands trembling, I picked up the glass.

"Just hold your nose and swallow it back," he said.

I glared at him, but did as he said. With one swift motion, I swallowed back half the glass in one gulp. Closing my eyes, I tried to ignore the revolting taste. I was about to swallow down the rest of the glass when I doubled over, coughing. I retched all the blood I'd just swallowed onto the floor.

It was completely involuntary, as though my body was having an allergic reaction to it. I leaned against the back of the chair, my mother wiping my mouth with a towel. When I looked up at them, both were looking at me with concern.

"I can't drink that stuff," I breathed, before retching again. "I... I need proper blood. Human blood."

I could barely believe the words spilling from my own mouth.

My parents exchanged worried glances.

"We can try injecting you with blood," my father said. "At least that will help to ease some of the burning."

"I'll go to Corrine's medical room in the Sanctuary and fetch some equipment," my mother said and hurried off out of the door.

I groaned, sinking into a chair, gripping my head in my hands. In addition to my burning insides, I now felt a splitting headache coming on.

My father sat down next to me, watching me silently.

I looked up at him. "Is this normal?" I managed, clutching my abdomen.

My father frowned. "Detesting animal blood is normal. Throwing it up isn't," he said bluntly.

I squeezed the sides of the table, another wave of hunger roaring through my stomach.

"And being injected with animal blood," I gasped, "it will make the burning stop?"

"The craving for human blood will remain, but the burning will calm down. It won't be as unbearable…"

He pointed to the jug of blood. "Why don't you try once more to stomach it while we're waiting for Mom to return?"

I shook my head. "No, I'll just wait—"

Barely had I finished my sentence when there was a knock at the door. I breathed out in relief. My father sprang to his feet and opened it. I turned my head, expecting to see my mother back already.

Instead, my eyes fell on four girls. Girls I recognized, but suddenly could not put a name to as a darkness settled over my eyes.

Two voices spoke at once amid giggling.

"We heard Ben has woken up."

"We wanted to say hi."

"Get the hell out of here!" my father bellowed.

He was about to close the door on them, but with speed I didn't understand, my foot lodged through the crack and before my father could even grab me to hold me back, I'd caught a girl—I didn't even have the sense to know which. I felt her squirming beneath me as I brought her to the ground. A split second later, my fangs found her neck. Her screams in my ear only added to my frenzy as her warm blood began to gush into my mouth, dripping down my throat like smooth, sweet ecstasy. Finally, the satisfaction I'd been seeking ever since I'd first woken as this beast.

It was a struggle to even feel the guilt amid the waves of pleasure crashing over me. It was only once my father managed to pry me off the girl that I realized what I'd done.

I'd just claimed my first life.

The life of my ex-girlfriend, Yasmine Renner.

Chapter 17: Derek

I could hardly believe my eyes. I was hoping that somehow this was a dream. That I'd wake up and Ben would still be locked safely in his bedroom. And yet here I was, a young woman's blood soaking my hands, staring at deep wounds in her neck caused by my own son.

At first I hoped there might be some hope of saving her. But I soon realized that she was cold in my arms.

"No," I breathed. "No."

It was the third human casualty within the space of a few days, after we'd gone years without a single violent death on the island.

The girl still lay on the floor of our apartment in a pool of her own blood. My first priority had to be getting my son away from the other girls still standing outside the door, shellshocked at what they'd just witnessed. I hurled myself at him, dragging him back toward his room. He gave no resistance. Blood still dripped from his lips and stained his clothes. His face was ashen as he stared at the body on the floor, his breathing harsh and uneven.

Ben's expression reminded me too much of the first time I'd killed.

The rush. The pleasure. The horror.

Pushing Ben back into his room, I locked the door before racing back into the hallway. I glared at the girls.

"Leave now," I said hoarsely.

All the blood had drained from their faces, and they lost no time in scampering away. Looking down once again at the corpse, I cursed beneath my breath. We knew Yasmine's parents personally. *How will we ever tell them?*

As I wrapped the corpse up inside the blanket it rested on, I heard a gasp behind me. I looked up to see

Sofia, hand clasped over her mouth.

"No," she breathed, kneeling down next to me and staring at Yasmine's corpse. "No."

Brushing Sofia's hands away from the rug, I proceeded to wrap Yasmine up. I carried her outside and laid her down outside on the veranda.

"Where is Ben?" Sofia choked.

I nodded my head toward the direction of his bedroom and she hurried away.

I cast my eyes around the bloodstained room. We'd been worried about werewolves attacking our humans. Now we had to concern ourselves first and foremost with protecting them from our own son.

I stared at the medical equipment Sofia had brought in and dropped on the floor as soon as she'd seen the corpse. Then my eyes fell on the jug of blood we'd tried to feed Ben, still perched on the kitchen table.

In a fit of rage and frustration, I grabbed the jug and smashed it against the counter. Blood soaked the surface, dripping down to mix with Yasmine's on the floor.

Chapter 18: Rose

When Annora still hadn't returned by the afternoon, Caleb went looking for her again. He returned a few hours later, unsuccessful.

Truth be told, I was expecting him to look more worried than he did as he swung back up onto my branch. While he certainly looked concerned, I wondered if he also was secretly hoping something had happened to her. It would relieve him of the responsibility he seemed so bent on having for her. It would be an easy way out.

"I wonder if she perhaps saw us across the lake," he

murmured.

Oh, I so hope that she did.

"Perhaps," I said. "I have a feeling she'll return though."

He sat down on the bunk next to me. Reaching for my hand, he planted a kiss on the back of it. My cheeks grew warm. I cleared my throat, leaning back against the truck of a tree and trying to make myself more comfortable next to him. I ought to make the most of this time I had alone with Caleb. I didn't know when Annora would return and then how long it would be before we had time without her.

"So, Caleb Achilles..." I threw him a sideways glance. "It seems you have a type."

He raised a brow at me, a small smile curving his lips.

"Tall, long black hair..." I continued, unable to hold back a grin.

He rolled his eyes, but indulged me. "Perhaps I do," he said. "But I'd need more of a track record for you to conclude that."

"Was Annora your first?"

He nodded.

"And… what number am I?"

"I'm not sure I feel comfortable placing a number on you, princess." He twined his fingers with mine. "But if you're asking if there was anyone between Annora and you, the answer is no."

He reached for me suddenly, pulling me back against his chest. He ran his fingers through my hair, pulling my head backward until the base of my head touched his collarbone. He was so strong, it felt like he could snap my neck in two. His rough cheek brushed against my face and settled near my neck.

"What about you, Rose Novak? Do you have a type?"

I felt heat rise in my cheeks again.

The truth was, I'd never really had a crush before Caleb. Sure, I'd met boys I'd thought were cute. But never the heart-stopping, all-consuming passion I felt for Caleb.

"I… I don't know."

He loosened his grip, his eyes fixing on me intensely. His expression was suddenly serious as he studied every flicker of emotion that crossed my face.

"What do you mean?"

"You're my first."

His eyes softened, and he looked at me like I was the most precious thing in the world. As though those three words I'd just spoken had made me seem fragile, vulnerable.

"Why do you look so surprised?" I asked, trying to break up his seriousness with a grin.

He ran a hand through his hair. His lips parted, then closed again. I didn't understand what had rendered him so speechless.

"Are all the young men in The Shade blind?" he said finally, staring at me incredulously.

I laughed. "No. But I'm not the only girl there. I guess it also doesn't help being the daughter of the most intimidating vampire on the planet."

Caleb fell silent. I reached my hands around his neck and brought his head down so I could place a kiss on his lips. It had been a mistake mentioning my father. Caleb always fell silent and grew serious when he turned his thoughts to him.

Realizing that I was hungry, I reached for a coconut in the corner of the bunk and attempted to smash it open against a nearby branch. After my third failed attempt, Caleb took the coconut from me and split it open with the pressure of his hands alone.

"Thanks," I muttered as I took the two halves from him. He reached for a long sharp leaf and helped me to loosen the flesh from the shell.

"Shall I feed you while I'm at it?" he teased.

He was joking, but I took him up on his offer all the same. I slid down his chest until my head rested on his lap, opening my mouth in expectation. He smiled, then slid the first piece of flesh into my mouth.

I stared up at him as I chewed. I brushed my hand against his strong jawline, tracing my fingers over his rough stubble.

As he slid the last piece of flesh into my mouth, I caught his hand before he could draw it away, pulling his thumb toward my mouth. I sucked on it, then gently dug my teeth into it.

Moving the coconut shells aside, I sat up and, holding his shoulders, pushed him backward. He had a questioning look in his eyes, but leaned back as I was requesting. Placing my legs either side of his hips, I crouched down over him. I lowered my head down to his neck, kissing his cheek along the way. I pressed my mouth against his throat and grazed my teeth over his cool skin.

"What are you doing?" he asked, amusement in his voice.

"Practicing being a vampire," I whispered back.

His chest shook as he chuckled.

The moment he chuckled, I wanted to look into his eyes. They lit up on the rare occasions that he laughed. I lifted myself up, still sitting on top of him, and spread my palms out over his chest.

I'd already decided that when the time came for me to turn into a vampire, I wanted Caleb to do it. I didn't dare mention it now though. He'd have to get over the trauma of his turning Annora first before I even dared bring up the subject with him. He was still far too broken from that experience. He'd been afraid he might ruin me just by kissing me back on the boat. At least we seemed to be past that stage. He seemed comfortable being close and intimate with me now.

Though there were still boundaries I knew he wasn't yet ready to cross. And I had to be careful not to make him feel uncomfortable about that.

Caleb's arm shot out toward a nearby tree. When he

withdrew it, he was holding a large purple hibiscus. My heart fluttered as he brushed the hair away from the side of my face and tucked it behind my ear.

I lifted myself off him and lay down by his side, positioning myself so that my face was level with his. He had discarded his ripped shirt by now, and wore only his pants. It pained me to see all the scars he still had from the bullets he'd endured back in Brazil and Venezuela. I could even see the dark shadow of many of them beneath his skin.

Caleb Achilles. My beautiful, broken warrior.

We lay in silence for the next few minutes as both of us became serious. We just lay there, staring into each other's eyes. When he finally did break the silence with a husky whisper, it let loose a thousand butterflies in my stomach.

"You're beautiful, Rose Novak."

If only Annora would just vanish, I could happily spend the next few years alone on this island with Caleb.

Chapter 19: Annora

I climbed up onto the edge of the old cracked well, staring down into the starry black abyss. I was almost sucked down instantly. Drawing a deep breath, I leaped into the gate.

I twisted and turned in the void as I rushed downward at what felt like the speed of light. I barely had time to be nervous at what might be waiting for me on the other side. Which was a good thing. I couldn't afford for them to detect apprehension in me.

I braced myself as I detected the light at the end of the tunnel. Placing my hands over my chest to cover myself, I finally shot out of the tunnel, landing in a heap. I scrambled to my feet as soon as I could, adjusting the leaves around my waist to cover as much of me as possible and bunching my hair over my chest.

I took in my surroundings. I was standing on a long, wide beach. Ocean stretched out in front of me for as far as the eye could see. Behind me was a towering stone wall. Behind it, I could make out the peaks of the massive black mountain ranges that this realm was famous for. My eyes traveled along the wall, and rested on a giant iron gate, spiked with human skulls.

I drew in a deep breath. I had only been to the realm of the ogres once before and it was a memory I would not easily forget. I'd gone with Isolde, to accompany her on a negotiation. The black witches would supply ogres with humans in exchange for their own kind's blood, which was the ingredient of many rituals we carried out, along with some other favors.

Although I'd known about this trade between the ogres and the witches for a long time, I had never been directly part of it since that meeting and I hadn't known exactly where the gate to the ogres' realm was located on earth. It was such luck that Caleb had led us all right to their primary point of trade.

I realized with a shudder that it was likely some black witches had also been present that night we heard the screams, to carry out the exchange through the gate.

Brushing the sand off my body, I tried to get my thoughts in order. I knew the king and queen of this island would recognize me from all those years ago. And if I played my cards right, they would have no reason to suspect I was without magic now. Ogres both feared and revered black witches. I would have to play on this knowledge if I was to get what I wanted. I knew how dangerous it was to invoke the order of the black witches fraudulently. But right now, the vision of Rose and Caleb embracing across the lake still fresh in my mind, I was willing to risk the consequences. I was in trouble with the black witches anyway if they found out about my helping Rose and Caleb escape Julisse and Arielle. One more notch on my reputation wouldn't make a whole lot of difference to the punishment I would undergo should they ever catch me.

I snapped myself back to reality. I was standing here topless, with nothing but a breaking wreath of leaves around my waist. I had to somehow make myself presentable before entering the ogres' kingdom…

I scanned the shoreline once more and noticed a cluster of small boats in the distance. I ran up to them as fast as I could and peered into the first one. It was empty. As were the second and third boats. When I climbed aboard the fourth boat—about twice the size of the previous three—I finally found something I could work with. A large black cloak—belonging to an ogre no doubt—rested over the back of a chair. It was so heavy my arm muscles felt strained just picking it up and so long it dragged along the floor behind me.

I walked to the cabin at the front of the ship, rummaging around in a large chest a few feet away from the giant wheel. I found an array of weapons—daggers, swords, axes… I picked up the sharpest dagger I could find. Laying the cloak down on the ground, I used the knife to shorten it to my height.

I pulled it over me. Although it looked baggy around my chest, this would have to do for now. I tried to tidy up the hems so that it looked less obvious that I'd just cut it with a crude knife. But then I had no more time to spend on this.

I threw the excess cloth over the edge of the boat into

the sea, replaced the dagger in the chest and then left the vessel. I raced back toward the wall, my eyes fixed on the nightmarish iron gates.

The gates of hell, they were often called. For, as the saying went: *He who ventures in doesn't venture out.*

My breathing quickened as I reached the gates. What I was about to do would be suicidal if any of the ogres found out, or somehow knew already, that I was a rogue witch. Their belief that I was still with the black witches would be the only thing keeping them from frying my insides for dinner.

I tried to tame my long hair a bit, brushing through it with my hands and winding it into a tight bun at the top of my head. Then I ducked down and, picking up a rock, slammed it against the iron three times. The eerie sound of the echoing metal sent shivers running down my spine.

My mouth dried out as I waited, my stomach churning.

I prayed that the royals would remember me from my visit before. I hoped I didn't look too different now that I was a human.

My heart leapt into my throat as the clank of a bolt

being drawn broke through the silence. The gates creaked open slowly until I stood face to face with a bulging ogre who looked almost five times my size. His bright yellow eyes glinted as he stared at me, frowning.

I spoke before he could come to too many assumptions of his own about my presence.

"My name is Annora. I am on commission here from Rhys and Isolde. In service of the order of our Ancients, I am here to see His and Her Highnesses."

His eyes widened the moment I mentioned Rhys and Isolde. He grunted, beckoning me forward. While ogres generally despised the witches of The Sanctuary, mention of the order of the black witches was enough to invoke reverence and fear in this guard.

I entered through the gates, burying my hands within the robe to hide the way they were shaking.

"Their Highnesses usually rest at this time, after lunch. But I will see if Anselm is awake," the ogre boomed into my ear.

Anselm. I racked my brain to remember who he was. Of course, I couldn't ask. I needed to appear as knowledgeable about these ogres as possible. So I nodded, despite the fact that I had no idea what I was about to walk into.

"May I carry you, witch? It will be faster."

Eyeing the grotesque ogre, I nodded. "You may."

"Or, of course, you could simply magic us inside, if you are familiar with the castle."

"I am not so familiar with the exact location," I said. "It's better if you carry me."

"As you wish," he mumbled.

He reached down his hand and laid it flat on the floor like a step. I stepped onto it, and he lifted me up to lean against his shoulder as he began thundering forward. My heart pounded in my chest as he sped up to an even faster pace. I hoped he wouldn't wonder why I was barefoot. I would try to hide my feet with the hem of my cloak when I was presented before this Anselm, whoever he was.

We traveled along a dirt path, lined either side by gnarled black trees, which led into a clearing filled with tombstones. The royal graveyard. I remembered passing by this before. The foot of a mountain lay up ahead. There was a massive wooden door at its base. The ogre drew keys from his pocket and pushed the doors open. Chilly air crept down my neck as he entered the base of the mountain and locked the doors behind us.

We passed through one cavernous hall after another. The walls were lined with long, blood red and deep orange tapestries depicting various pastimes of their ancestors of old. Mostly involving consumption of human flesh.

I was beginning to lose track of how many chambers we had traveled through when the ogre finally stopped and set me down on the ground.

"Please wait here."

Turning his back on me, he walked up to a door to our right and knocked. It swung open after several seconds. I couldn't see who was behind the door because the guard's imposing form was blocking my view.

"You have a visitor. A black witch. Her name is Annora."

There was a pause before a deep male voice said, "Show her in."

The guard stepped aside to reveal a tall figure, his face cast in shadow. I stepped into a grand high-ceilinged hall whose walls were covered with rich velvet tapestries. Now that Anselm had turned around, in the light of the torches, I was better able to make out his face and I immediately realized who he was. He was almost a splitting image of his father. He was the prince of this kingdom.

As he was royalty, his features and physique were very different from any usual ogre's. His frame was tall, muscular but slender. While he had brown leathery skin, his facial features were more humanoid. His nose was thin and straight, his jawline sharp, and he had no tusks. He had a regal appearance and I found him almost handsome.

"Annora." He bowed his head, reaching out a strong hand. "A pleasure to meet you."

I shook his hand.

"Come sit."

I followed him to the end of the hall where there was a long table and high-backed, cushioned chairs. He drew one up for me and took a seat opposite me. He reached for a jug of blood and filled two goblets.

Now that I was a human, the idea of drinking blood was vile. I wasn't even sure what type of blood this was—human, I suspected, since that was a favorite of the royals'. I couldn't make him suspect anything was different about me, so I took a polite sip of the cool liquid before setting the goblet back on the table.

"What brings you here?" He flashed me a charming smile, revealing a set of surprisingly white teeth.

"On behalf of my fellow witches, and to thank you for your loyalty all these years, I have come to offer a rare gift to your majesties. A human girl whose blood is one of a kind. It will taste unlike anything you've had before."

Anselm looked at me expectantly. "Well, where is she?"

"She is in the human realm, waiting for you on the island we use to trade. Not far from the other side of the gate."

He frowned. "Why didn't you bring her with you now?"

I gave him a gracious smile. "Well, you see, this young woman really is quite a beauty. If you have room in your harem, before you taste her, I was thinking she would make an exquisite addition."

He smirked. "My father and I always have room in our harem."

I chuckled. "I thought as much. Then you can

understand why I wanted to leave capturing her to you. I know you royals enjoy the chase…"

He licked his lips, his deep orange eyes gleaming.

"Indeed we do."

CHAPTER 20: ROSE

Annora still hadn't shown up by the time night fell. Although we'd stayed around base camp in case she returned, we both wanted to take a bath before sleeping. We climbed down the tree and walked to the edge of the lake.

My mouth fell open as Caleb dropped his pants on the grass. He dove in and resurfaced in the water, flicking his hair back and looking up at me. He cocked his head to one side.

"What are you waiting for?"

Apparently too impatient to wait for my answer, he

climbed out onto the bank and stood up. My cheeks ablaze, I kept my eyes fixed on his face as he approached me. He fingered my bra straps.

"This thing is filthy," he said, looking it over disapprovingly.

Before I could respond, he reached around my back and unclasped my bra. He'd already seen what I looked like on the boat, but I still found myself blushing as his eyes roamed me. There was a warmth in his eyes as he smiled at my bashfulness. He caught my hand, pulling me toward the water. Scooping me up in his arms, he leapt, submerging both of us in the cool water.

I resurfaced, gasping for breath. Since my panties were half off already from the contact with the water, I just discarded them completely too. I threw them on the bank near my bra.

Caleb resurfaced a foot away from me, reaching out and pulling me against him. I shivered as his palms began running up and down against my skin, scrubbing me like a sponge. He breathed deeply into my neck.

"You always smell good to me," he whispered.

I couldn't help but giggle at that. "Would I still smell good if Annora dropped a pile of bird poop on me?"

He laughed, and I once again found myself looking up into his gorgeous brown eyes. They sparkled as they reflected the moonlight hitting the water.

"I guessed that was you," he muttered, looking at me with mock disdain.

I considered pointing out that the crap and the spider were both a light punishment considering she'd tried to burn me alive in the submarine. But I was in too good a mood to bring up that traumatic incident.

I twisted around and began to run my hands along his muscular arms and shoulders, taking my turn to wash him. I swam toward the bank and grabbed a handful of clean grass. Bunching it up, I used it to scrub his skin. It was more effective than my palms, which weren't rough like Caleb's. I moved round to his sculpted back. When he felt me slowing down around the areas he had bullets embedded, he said, "It's okay. Those parts are numb. They don't hurt."

Once I'd finished making my way around his body, I let go of the grass.

"Thank you, Princess," he whispered, gathering me to him and claiming my lips.

"A-Any time," I replied breathlessly.

My body responding to his touch, I shivered again. Mistaking my pleasure for coldness, he sped forward and carried me out of the water, back onto the bank.

That was the thing with vampires—there was barely a second to object between the time they made a decision and the time they executed it.

Still, with images of spending the night with Caleb in his bunk floating around in my head, I didn't mind too much leaving the water so soon.

Gathering up my dirty underwear, I bent over the water and scrubbed them clean before laying them out on a stone to dry.

I dried myself with the shawl Caleb had found earlier. I turned around to see Caleb ripping off leaves from a cluster of bushes nearby. I walked over to him, eyeing him questioningly. He'd found the ripped pair of pants I'd discarded on the bank the day before and, removing the elastic from the waist, began to string it through the broad leaves to form a skirt.

I watched with fascination as his nimble fingers completed the garment. He looked up at me, beckoning me closer. He tugged away the shawl I was holding around my body and wrapped the skirt around my waist before knotting the elastic at the side.

I was impressed. It was long enough to make me feel comfortable wearing it, but not so long as to get in the way. The leaves were also softer than I'd imagined they would be. They felt almost velvety against my skin.

Using the piece of elastic he had left over, he began stringing it through two more broad leaves. Then he stood up, kissing me deeply as he reached around me and adorned my chest with the bikini.

"Wow," I said, eyeing the complete result once I'd recovered from his kiss. I looked at him. "And what about you?"

I could see he'd been so absorbed in thinking about my own modesty that he hadn't yet stopped to consider his.

He cast his eyes around the bank, an amused look on his face. "Do you think a skirt would suit me?"

I laughed. "Um. Probably not."

He furrowed his brows. "Then what do you suggest I wear until my own pants dry?"

Still giggling, I picked up my torn pants. There was no elastic left in them, but we could use the fabric to string something together... I picked some more of the velvety leaves he'd used for my bikini.

"Can you rip three long strips off the fabric with your nails?"

He did as I'd requested and handed them to me. My skills weren't as impressive as his, but after a few minutes I'd managed to fashion him something half decent.

I held it up to him.

"How about a loincloth?"

He grimaced as he took it from me and fastened it around his waist.

"Sexy," I said, giggling as he finished putting it on.

He rolled his eyes.

"How does it feel?" I asked.

"Stupid."

I laughed harder. At least it was better than a skirt.

Picking up his own pants, he walked over to the water and washed them, laying them out to dry on a stone near where I'd left my underwear.

Then, bending down so I could get onto his back, he carried me back to the foot of our tree and climbed with me up to his bed.

I climbed up first, crawling to the edge to make room

for him. He was about to follow when the inevitable finally happened. Annora returned.

Caleb's and my eyes shot downward as we heard the creaking of a branch. I groaned internally as her dark head approached closer and closer until she had reached our level. Since she'd found me about to climb into Caleb's bed, I expected her to throw me a deep scowl. She didn't. She barely even looked at either of us as her eyes fixed on her clasped hands.

Caleb slipped off his bunk and stood up, staring down at her. "Where were you?"

Her voice was deep and cracked as she responded. "I thought we needed a time out… I needed some space to think about things."

Caleb and I exchanged glances. He looked as confused as me.

"What do you mean?" he asked.

Annora sighed deeply before finally raising her eyes to his.

"I've been thinking about you, about me… about Rose. First, I need to apologize to you, Rose." Her gaze fell on me. "I was the one who set the submarine on fire."

I gaped at her. Caleb exhaled sharply.

Why would she admit to that?

"I was so blind with jealousy seeing the affection Caleb held for you. I wasn't thinking straight. I'm not sure that you'll ever forgive me, but I'm sorry."

She leaned back against a tree, clutching her left arm. Caleb and I remained speechless. "It's not fair that I resent either of you. I neglected Caleb for many, many years. I can't just expect things to be the same as they were." Her voice trembled, and I thought she was about to break down, but she swallowed hard and continued. "I'm going to step back."

I could barely believe my eyes as she gripped the engagement ring on her finger, pulled it off and handed it to Caleb. She had tears in her eyes as she looked at him, her chest heaving. "It's better you have this back." She reached for his hand and closed his fingers over the ring.

Then she turned to me again, placing a hand on my shoulder. "I won't get in your way again. And I'm sorry for all the harsh words I spoke to you earlier. You didn't deserve them. I just needed the time I spent apart to clear my brain and think things through. And as I did, I realized I felt like a monster for my behavior… So again, I'm sorry. I wish the two of you happiness. I'll no longer be in your way. I suppose we'll have to try to find a way to get off this island. When we do, you can drop me off somewhere and I'll… I'll try to start a new life away from all this supernatural craziness. Perhaps, in a few years, I'll meet a new sweetheart of my own."

Caleb's mouth opened and closed, but no words came out. I was sure I looked like a drowning fish too as I tried to understand what game she was playing with us now. It felt like she'd just had a personality transplant. Or been possessed.

Eventually it was Caleb who managed to break the silence. "Annora, I… I'm glad you've come to this conclusion by yourself." He paused, eyeing her steadily. "Because I can't lie. What we had is gone. It died over the years we spent together in that frozen castle… I don't love you any more."

Her jaw twitched, tears looking dangerously close to falling. I expected to see at least some hint of jealousy or anger toward me. But I saw nothing but sadness and regret.

He gripped her shoulder. "Once we manage to get

off this island, we'll take you to the nearest shore and find you somewhere to stay. A hostel, a shelter for the homeless. You can start your life over and stay out of trouble."

She nodded, then turned away and began climbing back down to her bunk.

I stared at the ring in Caleb's hands, dumbstruck.

While every part of me wanted to believe that Annora had changed, somehow, I just could not believe it. I didn't know what game she was playing, what this new change of tack was, but I didn't like it.

It was somehow more unsettling than when she had challenged me outright.

Chapter 21: Aiden

Even though we still hadn't managed to locate the bodies of Caroline and Thomas, we held a joint ceremony for them along with Yasmine. Yasmine's parents were inconsolable. Derek and Sofia did all they could to apologize—but what were words in the face of the loss of one's child? The death of Caroline and Thomas, and now the death of Yasmine, all within such a short period, sent shockwaves throughout the community of humans.

I'd noticed humans keeping to themselves more and eyeing vampires warily as they passed by. It seemed they'd developed a distrust of all supernatural creatures. This was something that used to happen in the old days of The Shade, before humans were made equal. To see us regressing toward such a state of distrust in such a short space of time was disturbing.

I looked around the moonlit courtyard outside the Sanctuary where we had gathered for the ceremony. The crowd of vampires seemed thinner than it should have been. Some of the most familiar faces were absent. There were a large number of humans attending—albeit sticking to one corner. There were also werewolves, witches, and Brett, who was wearing a new waistcoat for the occasion.

Derek and Sofia stood opposite me, next to Kyle and Anna. I noted Mona, Kiev, Erik and Saira standing in front of me. Matteo and Helina were a few feet behind. Vivienne, Xavier, Corrine and Ibrahim were missing, of course, and Eli was still recovering from the injury I'd caused, being nursed by Adelle. I wondered if that was why it looked emptier... No. As I looked around, I realized that six of our key council members were missing: Claudia and Yuri; Landis and Ashley; Gavin and Zinnia. As council members, they of all people should have been present.

As Yasmine was lowered into a grave by her parents and the ceremony came to a close, the crowds began to disperse. I walked up to Derek and Sofia, both looking far paler than even vampires should. Sofia had tearstains down her cheeks and her eyes were red from crying.

I wasn't sure if there was anything I could say that could console her. So I didn't bring up the subject of Yasmine. Instead I asked the question that had been nagging me.

"Why were so many vampires missing?" I asked.

Sofia looked so anxious, I wouldn't have been surprised if she'd barely noticed. Derek, however, shared my concern.

"It's odd that they would all be missing at once," he said.

"Leave it to me," I replied, pulling my cloak closer against me. "I'll investigate."

They had enough on their plate already. This was the least I could do to help.

Since Gavin and Zinnia's home was nearest to the Sanctuary, I decided to stop by there first. I leapt up to their treehouse and knocked three times on the door.

A ginger-haired lad, Rose's best friend, Griffin, answered the door. Worry marred his face and he could barely find it in himself to smile at me.

He raised a brow. "Aiden?"

"Where are your parents?"

He drew a sharp breath. "They're here. Locked themselves in either side of the apartment."

"Why weren't they at the funeral?"

He grimaced. "They… they've had a fight."

"Oh. I… I'm sorry to hear that… Now's not a good time then."

Griffin shook his head grimly.

I retreated and allowed him to close the door.

Gavin and Zinnia were known to have their disagreements. But from the look on Griffin's face, I sensed that this was worse than usual.

I descended the tree and continued through the forest until I reached my next stop—Landis and Ashley's tree. I stopped dead in my tracks as I reached the veranda. Ashley was sitting on the floor, leaning against the wall, sobbing into a tissue.

I felt awkward encroaching on her during such a private moment. But she noticed me before I could retreat, so I found myself walking over and kneeling down on the floor next to her.

I placed a hand on her shoulder as she sobbed even harder.

"Ashley, what's wrong?"

"Landis… he… he's cheating on me."

"What?"

"I saw him with one of the human girls."

I was stunned speechless as I stared at her. "Ashley, are you sure?"

She nodded vigorously.

"I mean, are you one hundred percent positive? You definitely saw Landis? Are you sure it couldn't have been someone else?"

"I have freaking vampire vision, Aiden. I know what I saw. It was him." Her sobbing became harder and she stood up abruptly, running back into her apartment and slamming the door behind her.

What is going on?

As I descended the treehouse and made my way toward the final couple, trepidation ate away at me thinking what I might witness there. I didn't know that I could stand seeing Claudia and Yuri fight. I'd grown too fond of them both.

As I reached their treehouse and began ascending, I could already hear an argument boiling up, the angry voice of Yuri drifting through the kitchen window. I didn't need to enter the home to hear what it was about.

I stopped outside the kitchen window and stared through it. Yuri and Claudia were standing at opposite ends of the room. Tears streamed down Claudia's face as Yuri shouted her down.

"I told you already, I didn't," Claudia cried. "I would never, Yuri. I swear—"

"Stop lying. Just stop it," Yuri bulldozed over her. "What do you take me for? A moron? I thought at least that much had changed when you married me. Now I see that I was wrong."

I couldn't believe such harsh words were coming from Yuri's mouth. He never spoke to her in this way. It was so unlike him.

Although it was none of my business, I couldn't stand watching my best friend crush his wife like this. I hurried to the front door and pounded my fists against it.

"Open up," I yelled.

The door swung open, Yuri standing there, his chest heaving as he glared at me.

"What do you want?" he spat.

Gripping his collar, I forced him back, away from the doorway, and barged into their apartment. I pushed him against the wall, pinning him there by his collar.

"Stop accusing Claudia of whatever it is you think she's done," I growled.

Yuri's eyes narrowed on me as he struggled against my grip. I held him there fast.

"Get off me!"

"Not until you listen to me."

He kneed me in the stomach, loosening my grip on him enough for him to scramble away from me. He rushed for the front door, but I got there before him, slamming it shut before he could exit. He exhaled in frustration, wiping sweat from his brow with the back of his hand.

"Listen to me, goddamn it!" I hissed. "You need to stop yelling at your wife before you sorely regret it. Something strange is going on around this island—"

Before I could finish my sentence, Yuri lurched for

one of the tall windows either side of the front door and smashed through it. Shards of glass fell everywhere. I tried to chase after him, but he slammed the elevator shut before I could reach it. I glared at him as he descended to the ground.

I walked back into the apartment toward the kitchen where Claudia was slumped in a chair, still sobbing uncontrollably. As I put an arm around her, trying to comfort her, I couldn't help but wonder.

Who's next?

Chapter 22: Sofia

Derek and I were in our kitchen, about to pour ourselves a glass or two of blood for dinner when I heard our elevator creaking. I looked out of the window to see Abby hurrying toward our front door. I left the kitchen and opened it before she had a chance to knock.

Her palms were sweaty as she clutched my hands and pulled me out of the penthouse.

"What's wrong, Abby?"

"There's been another one," she panted.

"Another what?" Derek had appeared at the door behind us.

"A killing."

My heart sank to my stomach.

"Who? Where?" Derek demanded. His face was stony as he grabbed his cloak and locked the front door behind us.

"Just... just come."

Derek had no patience for elevators, and neither did I. The three of us jumped off the balcony into a nearby tree and leapt from branch to branch down to the ground. Abby led us away from the Residences, toward the Vale. As we began winding through the streets toward the town square, I prayed that it wasn't Anna and Kyle this time. Whatever predator this was had struck just next door to them last time.

I was relieved when Abby led us straight past their house. We sped down several more streets before finally stopping in a cul-de-sac. She pointed to a house at the end of it where a crowd had gathered.

The crowd parted for Derek and me as soon as they noticed us. I looked around at the humans as we passed. Their faces were grim, their eyes filled with panic.

We entered the house, passing by more humans in the corridor and on the staircase. I held my breath as

Derek and I entered the bedroom at the top of the stairs.

It was a scene that belonged in a horror movie, much like the last incident. Clearly, this was the same predator. The sheets were soaked with blood and fragments of organs were sprayed about the room. As much as blood was delicious to me, even I found myself retching at this sight.

Again, there were no bodies.

Derek and I scanned the room and the ensuite bathroom. Derek turned to Abby, who had followed us upstairs.

"The whole house has been searched for remains?" he asked.

She nodded, swallowing hard. "What you see in this room is all we've found."

My husband and I stared at each other.

"How could there be no skeleton at least?" I breathed.

He clenched his jaw. "Either this predator is swallowing them whole, or we aren't looking hard enough for the remains."

"Then we need to double our efforts in searching this

island," I said.

Derek nodded, running a hand through his hair as he took in the ghastly sight once more before heading toward the exit. "And from this moment on, a vampire must be appointed to guard each human residence," he said while we descended the stairs. "No human home can be left unprotected until we get to the bottom of this."

As we walked out the front door, back onto the street, the crowd assailed us with question after question. Derek looked in my direction. I nodded, indicating that he should leave to make emergency arrangements while I remained to try to pacify our people.

I looked around at all the terrified and confused faces. I did my best to answer their questions. Most of all, they just wanted to be reassured that their children would be able to sleep safely at night.

"Derek has just left to make sure this place is swarming with vampire guards. They will camp out here and will not leave until we have found the killer."

"But what if it's a vampire who's the killer?" a high-pitched voice called out.

I looked toward the source of the voice, a young boy with jet-black hair. Cal was his name, if I remembered correctly. The youngest of the Anderson family. I walked up to him and placed a hand on his shoulder, bending down to his level so I could look him in the eye.

"No guard has touched a human on this island for almost twenty years, honey. Do you really think that one of them would have done this?"

He shrugged.

I looked around at the crowd again. Everyone surrounding me was also looking at me questioningly. It shocked me that this doubt could have entered so quickly into their hearts after we'd lived together in harmony on this island for so many years.

"What if it's Shadow?" a high-school student named Emily asked.

"Adelle has already confirmed that he was locked up in Eli's apartment during the time of the first attack. And both of these attacks were clearly carried out by the same killer. Besides, Shadow has been trained by Eli to be of no harm to humans. Like the other vampires, he hasn't touched a human in recent history."

"What if it's a werewolf?" Hector, an elderly man, spoke up. "Would you sentence it to death or banish it from the island?"

It. I winced at the way he referred our new residents.

I looked Hector right in the eye. "Whoever it is—werewolf, vampire, or something else—will be thrown off the island, never to return."

The werewolves were dear to Mona, but if one was proven to be a killer I was sure that even she would agree that he ought to be expelled.

"Will Benjamin be thrown out for murdering Yasmine then?"

My eyes shot toward the thirty-something brunette to my left, dressed in black. Angelica, Yasmine's aunt.

My voice caught in my throat. Several awkward moments of silence passed before I found my voice again.

"Angelica, the incident with Yasmine was a tragic accident," I said, fighting to keep my voice steady. "As you know, Benjamin had just come to after being turned and Yasmine showed up right on his doorstep—"

"So you blame Yasmine?"

I stared at her, horrified at the way she was twisting my words. "That's not what I said. I said that it was an accident. Yasmine was excited to see my son, who was not in control of himself. The deaths of Caroline and Thomas, and now Lucinda and Izmael, are clearly in a league of their own. They were no accident. They were cold-blooded murders."

"So if Ben was indeed found to be responsible for Caroline, Thomas, Lucinda and Izmael's deaths, you would classify him as a cold-blooded murderer?" Angelica shot back. She looked around at the crowd. "Remember our queen's words, people. We have this from her own mouth."

"My son did not kill them," I said through gritted teeth.

Angelica looked like she was about to throw another bitter retort, but, apparently satisfied that she'd done enough damage, she pursed her lips and began walking in the opposite direction.

"When will the guards arrive?" Hector asked after a pause.

"Within half an hour," I replied, relieved for the change of subject. "My husband is seeing to it as we speak."

The crowd mumbled among themselves and after answering the rest of their questions, I took my leave.

As I exited the Vale, my mouth was dry. The encounter with Angelica had shaken me, and I still hadn't recovered from it.

Ben couldn't have done this… could he?

I stopped in my tracks, shocked to realize that her words had instilled even the slightest bit of doubt in me about my son.

If even his own mother can't have complete conviction in his innocence, where does that leave The Shade's prince?

I shook the thought away, trying to dismiss all doubt that it could have been my son. I had almost reached the Residences when Patricia appeared out of thin air in front of me.

"We've found the killer."

My mouth dropped open. "Who?"

"The ogre."

Chapter 23: Sofia

"Brett?" I gasped, staring at Patricia in disbelief. "How would he even fit in those small human houses? He's far too big. It would have been imposs—"

"The evidence is quite conclusive," she said, looking at me sternly. "Just come with me."

She touched my shoulder and we vanished. We reappeared a few seconds later, standing on a flat boulder directly outside Brett's cave.

I was shocked to see that there was already a crowd of humans surrounding the area. How they had gotten wind of this before even I had was bewildering. The last thing I wanted was people to start doubting Brett before I'd even seen the evidence.

"Why are there so many people here already?" I demanded.

Patricia looked around at the crowd before turning back to me.

"The humans haven't been content with leaving the search to the witches. We were in the process of scouring the sea within the borders of the island when a group of humans called our attention to this…"

Gripping my arm, she pulled me over toward a gap in the rocks, about ten feet away. I looked down to see a mess of mangled limbs.

"Four bodies, all piled up and squashed into the same place," Patricia said, grimacing as she looked over the corpses.

"They were found in this spot exactly?"

"Yes," she said, looking back at Brett's cave. "Less than ten feet away from the ogre's home. The humans rolled a boulder away from them to gain a better view of them, but other than that they have not been touched. Assuming the humans aren't lying, of course. But I doubt that. It's more in their interest than ours to find the killer."

My insides writhed to see how slashed and squished the corpses were. They were unrecognizable. I could barely make out the start of one body and the end of the next. I covered my nose with the sleeve of my blouse, trying to block out the rotting stench.

"And where is Brett now?" I asked, casting my eyes toward the dark entrance of the cave.

"Sleeping."

I looked at the humans surrounding us again. They were all staring at us expectantly. From the looks on their faces, I was sure that they felt like storming the ogre's home with pitchforks already.

"Patricia," I said, turning my back on them to face her again, "you said you had conclusive evidence. Where is it?"

She raised a brow and nodded down toward the bodies.

I exhaled impatiently. "This is not conclusive evidence. Someone could have framed Brett, for all we know. Besides, you still haven't answered how he could have even gotten to those humans in the first place."

She heaved a sigh and bit her lip, shrugging. "Well,

it's the most conclusive we've found so far."

I brushed past her and looked down once again at the mangled bodies.

"At least we've found the corpses now," I muttered. "We have to hope that they are not too mashed up for us to examine. But in the meantime, nobody is to lay a hand on Brett. Not unless you or someone else can explain how he could have fit that elephantine body of his into those small homes—"

Barely had I spoken the words when a groan emanated from the cave. I whirled around and stared in horror as humans clambered up the rocks and began rushing inside.

I raced after them and, as I neared the back of the cave, gasped to see three humans already circling Brett, brandishing daggers. The ogre was slumped in a corner of his straw bed, grumbling and burying his head in his hands.

This sight alone should have been enough to convince anyone that Brett was not a killer. He could have smashed their skulls against the wall of the cave with a knock of his fist, but instead, he chose to cower in a corner.

The humans lowered their weapons as I stood in front of the ogre and glowered at them, but they still didn't put them away entirely.

"On what authority have you disturbed Brett?" I demanded.

"What authority do we need, Sofia?" one of the men spat. "Didn't you just see those bodies outside his cave? He has more than enough strength to mangle them into such a pulp."

"You need my or my husband's authority to lay a hand on any resident on this island, however guilty you may deem them to be," I shot back. "You all know the laws of The Shade, and if you don't, I suggest you lock yourselves indoors for a day and study them again to refresh your memory."

"Sofia, our lives are in danger—"

"Yes, but chasing down the wrong person isn't going to relieve that danger. Those bodies outside his cave prove nothing until we've examined them."

The crowd parted as a werewolf bounded into the cave. Saira. Her eyes blazed as she reached me and turned to face off the humans alongside me.

"Back off, people," she growled. "Brett has an alibi.

Me. I've been visiting every night for the past two weeks for bonfires on the beach."

Although Brett hardly needed an alibi—for the reason I'd already explained to Patricia numerous times—it could only help his case having one.

The men looked like they wanted to protest still—perhaps argue that Saira could be in on it too, since she was a werewolf—but with both Saira and I glaring at them, they sheathed their weapons and backed off.

"Go back to your homes," I said, ushering them all out of the cave. "If Brett reports any of you coming within a mile of his cave, you will answer to Derek Novak personally."

That made them pay attention. The blood drained from their faces and they scurried away like rats.

I sighed, looking back at Saira.

"Thank you for defending him, Sofia," she said. "He's more gentle a soul than any of those humans can ever hope to be."

"I guessed as much," I said.

"He has a phobia of violence. Wouldn't crack a person's skull even if you begged him to." She scowled, shooting a look back at the quivering ogre. "I should know. When we first accepted him as a member of our crew back in the supernatural realm, we thought he'd be useful helping us defend our ship... What did he do the first time a threat came along? He abandoned his post and went squealing below deck. The whole lot of us almost lost our damn lives because of it. After that, we trusted him with nothing but cooking and carving."

She smiled fondly. Padding over to the ogre, she nuzzled her head against his arm. Still, he refused to raise his head.

"It's okay, sweetie," she said. "You can look up now."

There was a pause.

"Are the meanies gone?" he mumbled.

Saira heaved a sigh, rolling her eyes at me. "Yes, the meanies are gone."

"They won't bother you again, Brett," I reassured him, walking up to him too and patting his heavy shoulder.

Saira remained with the ogre while I bade goodbye to both of them and left the cave. It was time for me to touch base with Derek.

Patricia was waiting outside the entrance as I emerged, still leaning over the bodies. She looked up at me questioningly.

"Take the bodies to the Sanctuary and, with the help of the other witches, start your examination. Report back to me or Derek once you've made some progress."

She nodded and, since she appeared to have no further questions, I took my leave. I ran across the boulders toward the beach and back into the forest. The events of the day replayed in my mind as I traveled.

Well, so far all we've done is establish who is not *the killer.*

But who on earth is?

Chapter 24: Rose

Despite my misgivings about Annora's motivations, she kept true to her word and stayed out of Caleb's and my way. She barely exchanged a word with either of us the next day. She went wandering off into the jungle by herself.

Caleb seemed to have his doubts too, but he was acting as though he believed her words. The idea of finally getting rid of Annora, dropping her off in some homeless shelter, leaving Caleb and I free to return to The Shade and discover for ourselves if anything had really happened there or if Hermia's words had been a lie, made me desperate to find a way off this island.

I sat on Caleb's bunk, looking around at the thick trees surrounding us. That was when it hit me. Caleb's trade used to be building ships. His father had been a shipyard owner.

"What if we built a boat?"

Caleb crossed his arms over his chest, looking around at the trees. "Absolutely from scratch," he muttered. "With not a single tool. I've never done anything like that before. But… I guess we've no choice but to try."

"Maybe there will be some parts of the submarine we can still use?" I said. "If we go to the wreck, and you dive down deep, maybe you can find some tools to make the job easier."

He nodded slowly. "Yes. There was a toolbox in the engine room. If that wasn't ruined in the blast, that could prove invaluable. Let's go and see if there's anything there that's salvageable."

Since Annora wasn't around, we couldn't warn her where we were heading off to. It would be tough luck if she arrived back and wondered where we'd gone.

It wasn't long before Caleb had rushed to the edge of the jungle. With the sun high in the sky, Caleb tore a branch with flat leaves off a tree nearby and held it over himself as he raced us toward the spot of the wreckage.

I took the branch from him as he set me down and continued holding it over his head as he entered the water. I followed him in as deep as I could still stand, and then, as he ducked beneath the waves, I stopped, waiting for him. I didn't know how much time I passed watching the surface of the water, waiting for him to emerge. But I breathed out a sigh of relief when he did. I hurried over to him, holding the leaf over him to shield him from the sun's harsh rays.

He was holding a large gray toolbox in one hand, while with the other he was clutching a thick metal sheet. We made our way back to the sand, where he dropped the items. I followed him back and forth from the sand to the sea as he retrieved more and more items for what felt like the next hour.

By the time he'd retrieved everything he deemed salvageable, the beach was covered with equipment. He dragged it all further inland, beneath the shade of the trees, so there was no chance of pieces being swept away.

Wiping sweat from his brow with the back of his

hand, he looked over the entire collection.

"Yes," he said quietly. "I think this might just work. We will only need a small boat. The smaller it is, the less likely things will go wrong and the faster I can build it." He began pacing up and down on the sand, thinking out loud. "We'll need wood... These coconut trees aren't as good as the trees surrounding our bunks."

He grabbed me and began hurrying back through the jungle. He stopped at our tree, pulled me up and set me down on his bunk. Annora still hadn't returned.

After planting a lingering kiss on my neck, he drew away. "It's safer if you stay up here while I work, out of harm's way. I'll come get you if there's anything you can help with. Otherwise just stay here for now... And if Annora returns, shout out and let me know. I still don't trust her alone with you."

I nodded, watching as he leapt back down the tree and jogged away further into the jungle.

Since I had nothing else to do, I decided to do some climbing. I made my way up to the top of the tree and looked out. The ocean was still crystal blue and empty for as far as I could see. There wasn't a single cloud in the blue sky. I breathed deeply, in and out, relishing the sea air and the warm sun tanning my skin. I imagined Caleb and I sailing away together on that crystal-blue sea, wrapped in each other's arms and kissing as we headed toward the sunset...

I lost track of time as I perched there, my head stuck out of the treetops, fantasizing and taking in the beauty surrounding me.

When something brushed against my ankle, I looked down in excitement, expecting to see Caleb.

Instead I was met with a vision that should have belonged only in a nightmare.

A brown leather-skinned man with glowing eyes and sharp white teeth gripped my ankle and pulled me downward.

Chapter 25: Caleb

A scream pierced through the jungle. I dropped my axe and hurtled back toward our tree.

I was sure that it was Rose's voice. It sounded so much like her. But when I stumbled across Annora lying on the ground, nursing a bleeding foot, I assumed that I must have been mistaken.

I bent down to take a closer look at it as she moaned and writhed. I held my breath as the scent of her blood invaded my nostrils. I gripped her foot, examining it. The flesh between her large and second toe had split. Blood was seeping from it, soaking the grass.

I slit open my palm and held it out to her. She gripped my palm, her soft tongue lapping up the blood. As the wound healed, I helped her up.

I decided to go check on Rose before I got back to work. I motioned to leave, but Annora tugged on my arm, pulling me back.

"I would also like to return to camp. Could you carry me? I don't want to cut myself again."

I allowed her to climb onto my back before running back toward our tree.

"Ouch."

I slowed for a moment, looking back at Annora. "What?"

"I didn't realize, I got a cut here too." She thrust out a bleeding wrist, hovering it barely an inch away from my nose. I almost dropped her as I tried to distance myself. My mouth was already watering from the blood on her foot.

Crouching over her again, I once again cut open my palm and fed her. I didn't dare pick her up again until the second wound had closed and she'd wiped her hands on her clothes to remove the excess blood.

"I need to get back now," I said impatiently as she

pulled herself onto me again.

She complained a couple of times that my speed was hurting her as I raced back to camp, but I ignored her. I was relieved to lower her to the ground once I arrived at the foot of the tree. Swinging myself up, I stopped at Rose's bunk, expecting to see her there, perhaps resting.

Her bed was empty.

"Rose?" I called, my heartbeat quickening.

I cast my eyes around, upward, downward, sideways, thinking perhaps she'd gone for a climb. She wasn't there. Perhaps she'd be by the lake, taking a swim to cool off during the heat of the day. She wasn't there either.

"Rose?" I yelled.

I raced through the jungle surrounding the tree, wondering if she'd ventured in search of more fruit, despite my requesting her to stay put. "Rose!" I bellowed, my heart hammering in my chest. I yelled until my throat was hoarse.

She can't have ventured this far barefoot. I haven't even been gone long.

There was another bloodcurdling scream.

Rose?

I whipped back through the jungle toward the source

of the noise, only to find Annora again. One palm was clasped over her mouth, the other shaking as she pointed a few hundred meters away from the foot of our tree.

My head reeled as I followed her gaze.

Lying in the undergrowth was a body.

No.

No.

Almost blind with panic, I rushed forward. As I approached, I found myself staring down at a corpse swarming with bees and so disfigured that, had it not been for her torn dark hair, I wouldn't even have known that it was Rose.

Chapter 26: Rose

The moment I screamed, the creature's leathery hand clamped my mouth shut. Withdrawing two silk handkerchiefs from his snakeskin waistcoat, he shoved one down my throat and, placing the other between my teeth, knotted it behind my head. It was all I could do to not vomit.

"Princess," he rasped in my ear. "I am most honored to make your acquaintance."

My struggling only broadened his smile as he began touching me in places not even Caleb had yet. He flung me over his shoulder and leapt from branch to branch down the tree. As his feet hit the ground, he launched into a sprint.

Everything had happened so quickly. I was still in shock. The jungle whizzed past me in a blur as blood rushed to my head. I tried to grab hold of a branch as we sped past one, but I only ended up cutting my palms as he hurtled forward regardless.

Then without warning, his grip around my ankles loosened and I crumpled to the ground, grazing my head against a sharp rock. In a daze, I scrambled backward until my back hit a tree trunk.

I looked up in horror at the creature staring down at me, a smirk still on his face.

"You want to run?" he said, licking his lips as his eyes roamed my almost bare body. "Now's your chance."

As I staggered to my feet, I picked up a rock. I hurled it at him and spun around, not even taking the time to see if it had hit its mark. Despite thorns and sharp leaves ripping through the soles of my feet, I couldn't allow myself to slow down. I cast a glance back over my shoulder to see he was still standing in the same spot. I ducked down behind a bush and then flung myself behind a nearby tree, slowly pivoting in a different direction to that which he had last seen me running in.

I tried to undo the gag so I could scream, but it was knotted so tight it would have taken me at least a few minutes. And I had no such time.

I heard the creaking of branches a few hundred meters away and froze behind the trunk of a tree. Peering round, I saw the creature approaching. I held my breath.

"I know who you are, treasure," he whispered through the trees. "But I ought to introduce myself. My name is Anselm Raskid. And we have something in common already. My parents are also king and queen... We are princess and prince."

I could barely pay attention to his words as he crept closer and closer. As he was seconds from discovering me, I picked up a thorny branch and, leaping out of my hiding pace, hurled it at the creature's face. He stumbled back. Reaching for a low-hanging tree branch, I fought to pull myself up onto it. I'd almost made it out of reach when his hand closed around my ankle. As he yanked me downward, to my horror, I found myself falling into his long, strong arms.

His face scratched and bloody, he seemed to have

had enough of whatever game he'd been playing as he wrestled me into submission and continued running with me through the jungle.

He only stopped again once we neared an old stone well. He leapt onto it, balancing us both on its narrow edge.

What in the world is he doing?

As I looked down into the hole, if my tongue hadn't been attached to the back of my mouth, I might have swallowed it.

Beneath us was a tunnel whose walls were made of what appeared to be a swirling light blue smoke. Beyond the walls was a black abyss, scattered with stars.

This was no well.

This was a gate.

Leading where, I was too terrified to even imagine.

As the creature prepared to jump, I caught sight of Annora standing a few feet away, half of her sweaty face cast in shadow. There was time to hear but a few words escape her lips before the beast and I hurtled downward:

"Annora Achilles. It has a nice ring to it, doesn't it?"

Chapter 27: Mona

It had been another long, stressful day. I'd managed to screen the entire island. There were no imposters. I would have sensed it the moment my spell touched them.

No. There had to be another explanation for the deaths. And this revelation left us with an even more chilling conclusion: it was one of our own who'd claimed their lives. Now that we'd found the bodies, hopefully it was only a matter of time before we found out who was behind it. I'd told Patricia and her team that they could call on me to help, but they seemed more than able to handle the job on their own.

I was relieved to return home. I went straight up to the bathroom, showered and then sat down in front of my dressing table, staring at myself in the mirror. I combed my hair and tied it up in a bun. My eyes fell on my mother's jewelry box. I fingered it absentmindedly as I tried to put a finger on the unease I'd felt over the recent days. Since the deaths, it felt like the whole island was riddled with tension... uncertainty... doubt. Vampires no longer trusted werewolves the way they once had, while werewolves felt wrongly accused by vampires. Witches, on the other hand, doubted both vampires and werewolves. And humans trusted no one. Then Ben had gone and murdered a human girl, causing many accusing fingers to point at him—the very prince of The Shade.

I hadn't experienced such strife since arriving in The Shade. I could see from Derek and Sofia's reaction that such turmoil wasn't commonplace here. They'd rebuilt the Shade based on trust and loyalty. That was how things had worked for almost two decades. A breakdown of trust would mean a breakdown of the whole structure. I didn't know what would follow if that happened.

Pushing the box back in its place in front of the mirror, I stood up and flopped down on the bed. Snuggling between the sheets, I wished that Kiev was home already. It was so late, I wondered where he could have gotten to.

I stayed awake for the next hour waiting for him, but when he still didn't return, sleep finally claimed me...

***

The cool evening breeze blew through my hair as I strolled through the woods. I didn't understand where Kiev could have gotten to. He almost always returned before this late hour. I worried that something might have happened to him.

I found myself exiting the woods and walking down toward the shore. I quickened my pace, scanning the beach as I went. It wasn't until I reached the end of the sand and approached a cluster of rocks that I noticed a light flickering in the room at the top of the lighthouse.

Could Kiev possibly be there? What would he be doing there at this time of night?

I climbed over the rocks toward the entrance and ascended the winding staircase. My heart was pounding in my chest as I finally reached the top. Reaching for the handle, I was about to open it, but realized that the door was already ajar. There was no need to disturb whoever was in there, in case it wasn't Kiev.

I knelt and looked through the crack.

My breath hitched.

There was Kiev, crouched down over the bare body of a woman whose face I could not see, for it was being showered with his kisses. But as my eyes fixed on the pillows beneath her head, I didn't need to.

It was Sofia's bare form writhing beneath him. Her deep red hair splayed out on the pillow. Her fingers dug into Kiev's back muscles as he pressed against her. His lips lowered to her pale neck. When he brushed his hands along her hips, tremors ran through his body.

They were so consumed with each other, it felt like I could have walked right over to them and they might not notice.

I couldn't remain a witness to this scene a moment longer.

Pushing the door open, I ran up to the bed. I gripped Kiev's shoulders, attempting to pull him off. But my fingers slipped off his skin like butter the moment I touched him.

I shouted. I screamed. I tried to use my magic to turn

over the bed.

But it was as if an invisible force field was around them, keeping them locked in their own little bubble. Nothing I did had any effect.

My shouting fell on deaf ears. My spells bounced off.

They still remained, lying there in a world of their own—a world I was totally locked out of. If anything, with all my attempts, their passion only increased each second that I stood there, until finally, Kiev whispered the words that sliced my heart in two:

"I have always loved you, Sofia."

***

My eyes shot open. Gasping for breath, I sat bolt upright. Beads of sweat dripped from my forehead. Shafts of moonlight trickled through the curtains, falling on Kiev's sleeping form beside me.

I dropped my head into my hands. It felt strangely chilly. From the sweat, I assumed.

I breathed deeply, trying to steady my racing heart.

It was a dream. Just a dream.

I lowered myself back down against my pillow and reached an arm around Kiev's waist, pulling myself closer against his back and kissing his shoulder as he remained in slumber.

Sofia would never betray me like that. She is my friend.

And Kiev certainly wouldn't.

In any case, he's over Sofia... isn't he?

CHAPTER 28: DEREK

The night had been plagued with... a strange dream.

After hours of tossing and turning, I eventually gave up trying to sleep and got out of bed. Making my way to the kitchen, I poured myself a glass of blood.

Trying to push aside thoughts of the nonsensical dream I'd had, I forced myself to think of the problems that were plaguing us.

As we had promised the humans, swarms of vampires were now taking turns to guard their homes. Sofia and I had also decided that we'd personally take a tour round the human residences three times a day to make sure everything was in order.

My thoughts turned to our son. Now that he had murdered Yasmine, humans, vampires, werewolves and witches alike had begun to suspect that perhaps he was the cause of the others' deaths too. Of course, Sofia and I knew that he couldn't have done it, but until we found the actual killer, this suspicion would remain in the hearts of many.

Ben. It had been a while since he'd last… fed. His blood levels would be running low again.

Grabbing some blood from the fridge and the syringe Sofia had fetched from Corrine's medical room, I headed to his bedroom.

Opening the door slowly, I was surprised to see that he was awake already. He lay flat on his back, staring up at the ceiling, his eyes glassy. He did nothing to acknowledge that I'd entered the room. I sat on the edge of the bed and reached for his collarbone. He didn't resist as I injected several doses of blood into him.

Then I left the room. I guessed he was feeling guilty about what he'd done. He didn't need me to rub it in. Silence was the best course of action right now. I made sure to lock the door behind me.

I retreated to my study and paced up and down for a while longer, mulling over the most urgent issues I had to do today, until eventually I decided to try to sleep again—at least for an hour before Sofia woke up at six o'clock, so we could wake up together.

But as I returned to our bedroom, she wasn't there. Her side of the bed had been neatly made, and her nightgown that had lain on the chair nearby was gone.

"Sofia?" I called softly.

I walked into the ensuite bathroom. It was empty. I walked back to the kitchen, thinking maybe she'd also had a restless night and was having some breakfast. But she wasn't there. I walked through the living room, intending to check some of the other rooms, when I noticed that her cloak that usually hung by the front door was gone, along with her set of keys fixed to the key holder near the door.

Then I spotted a sticky note on the door. Sofia's handwriting.

"Gone for a walk…"

An early-morning walk was appealing to me too, so I grabbed my coat and headed out. A brisk walk would do me some good, help to clear my thoughts for the day, and perhaps I'd even bump into Sofia.

I descended in the elevator and began walking through the woods. I wanted to feel the sea breeze against my skin and the water lapping around my feet, so I made my way toward the shore. But as I entered the clearing in front of the Port, I stopped short.

What I saw there, at the end of the jetty, made me believe that I must have still been dreaming.

Chapter 29: Mona

I tried to fall asleep again, but the nightmare kept resurfacing each time I tried.

I let go of Kiev and tossed and turned in bed, trying to find a comfortable position. I drifted off only briefly before being woken yet again by the same nightmare. I sat up in bed, rubbing my eyes.

I glanced down toward Kiev's side of the bed. It was empty now.

"Kiev?" I called.

I checked the bathroom and all the other rooms upstairs and downstairs. I could only assume he'd gone for a walk. Since I couldn't sleep, I decided I might as well go for a walk myself.

I exited the house and stepped onto the beach. I walked to the water's edge, dipping my feet in the waves. I looked out at the still dark horizon. The stars twinkled overhead, the moonlight making the sea glisten.

I wasn't sure where I was going. I just kept walking along until I eventually realized that I was nearing the island's port. I shifted away from the waves and moved further inland. It was only once I'd left the beach and climbed up the steps to the platform along which the subs were lined that I noticed two figures standing at the end of the jetty.

I had to look closely in the gloom—they could have almost been mistaken for one figure, they were embracing so tightly. I wasn't sure which lovebirds were making out at this time of the morning, and it felt intrusive to keep staring, so I was about to turn around and walk back toward home when I heard it.

A deep groan, and then a whisper—soft, but still clearly audible in the quiet of the early morning:

"Sofia."

I looked more closely, and now I could recognize Kiev's silhouette in the moonlight, and Sofia's long red hair.

I stared in horror.

This must still be a dream. I never woke up.

I was about to pinch myself when I heard the snapping of branches behind me. I whirled around to see the dark shadow of none other than Derek Novak. We both locked eyes. He looked as dumbstruck as I felt.

If Derek is here... witnessing exactly the same sight as me... how can this be a dream?

I looked back at Kiev and Sofia. His hands rested on her lower back, holding her flush against him as their lips kneaded against each other.

This isn't a dream.

I'm seeing this with my own eyes. This is happening.

I woke up. Kiev wasn't there. He'd come here... to meet Sofia.

My hands were shaking, my mind was on fire as doubt after doubt blazed through it.

Could my dream of them in the lighthouse have been a vision? Has it been Sofia on Kiev's mind whenever we've made love? Did he ever even love me? Was I just a distraction for him? How long have they been seeing each

*other since we arrived on the island? Is this why he wanted
to return here? For Sofia?*

I stumbled back further into the shadows of the trees.
Although my heart was burning, I didn't know that I
had the courage to hear it from his own lips. To hear
him admit that he loved Sofia over me. I didn't know
that I could handle the pain that would cause. I was in
enough agony already.

So I ran.

Vanishing myself away from the Port, I reappeared in
our bedroom.

Suddenly all the love, all the pleasure, I'd thought
we'd shared in this room together seemed to vanish into
an empty hole. I felt like I was losing my mind. All I
could see around me now were traces of the redhead.
Hell, I even thought that I could smell her here.

Anger coursed through my veins.

*All this time, both of them have been playing me for a
fool. I trusted them both, and they betrayed me in the worst
possible way.*

I felt fire heating up my palms, and as rage and grief
consumed me, I could no longer control it. Flames
burst from my fingertips, lighting up the bedsheets and
licking the walls until soon the whole room was

engulfed in the blaze. The heat was so scorching, tears could barely spill from my eyes before they dried out.

I looked around at the fire devouring the room. A room I'd once cherished. A room that now held nothing for me, except...

My eyes fell on my mother's jewelry box, still sitting on my dressing table. Its gems glimmered in the flames.

As I stared at that box, it suddenly felt like it was the only thing of value left for me on this deceitful island.

Chapter 30: Derek

The Port.

Where I'd shared my first kiss with Sofia.

Now where I saw—or thought I saw—my wife sharing a passionate kiss with Kiev Novalic.

Either the pressure I'm under has finally driven me to insanity, or I'm still dreaming.

Yet seeing Mona standing opposite me, sharing the same shocked expression—it somehow made the vision before me seem real. Another person could clearly see what I saw.

I was frozen to the spot. I could barely coordinate

myself enough to move my feet as I stared at my wife kissing Kiev as though her life depended on it.

Even when I was finally able to move and walk forward, I still couldn't find my voice. It was as though I'd swallowed my tongue, or forgotten I even had one.

As I reached the jetty and began walking toward them, Kiev caught Sofia's hand and they leapt off the edge. I couldn't see where to at first, but when I sped up, I caught sight of a submarine disappearing beneath the waves.

What?

I stood staring at the waves for several moments, blinking, trying to make sense of what had just happened.

"Derek?"

I didn't think that the night could become any more insane, but as I turned around to see Sofia running out of the forest toward me, I found myself reeling.

As she approached me wearing her nightdress, a bewildered look on her sleepy face, I looked from her to the water I thought I'd just seen her disappear beneath.

I reached out and gripped her arms, then caught her lips in mine. I kissed her hard, partly to make sure she was real and partly because I was still suffering from the torment of watching Kiev claim her.

"Derek," she gasped, as I finally let go of her. "What on earth is going on? What are you doing out of bed so early?"

I stared at her. My mind felt so muddled, I was unsure of how to even begin articulating my thoughts.

"I just saw you standing right here at the end of this jetty, kissing Kiev."

"What?"

"As I approached, you jumped down into a submarine and it submerged beneath the waves."

"Baby." She looked at me with concern in her eyes as she held my head in her hands. "What's happened to you? What's the last thing you remember before stepping outside?"

"I'd gotten out of bed to get a glass of blood and check on Ben. When I returned, you were no longer in bed. There was a note on the door, saying you'd gone for a walk. And then I reached the Port and saw you two…"

She reached up and placed a palm over my forehead, looking more worried than ever. "I felt you get up to check on Ben. And I was still in bed when you came back. I even spoke to you. You looked right through me as though I wasn't even there. Then you left the room and a minute later, I heard the front door opening and closing."

Before I even had a chance to process Sofia's words, someone called out to us.

"Derek. Sofia."

We turned to see Kiev jogging along the jetty toward us, still in his pajamas.

"Have you seen Mona?"

I was about to answer yes. But then I wondered if the vision of Mona had also been an illusion.

"I… I thought I saw her here, a few minutes ago."

Kiev frowned. "What do you mean, you thought you saw her?"

I exhaled in frustration. "Well, I also thought I just saw you making out with my wife."

Now it was Kiev's turn to look flummoxed. "What?" His eyes traveled from Sofia to me, then back to Sofia. "Has your husband been drinking?"

Sofia shook her head, though even she didn't seem so sure as she still looked at me worriedly.

"I haven't been drinking," I said impatiently. My head in my hands, I closed my eyes, leaning against the railing, trying to make sense of my thoughts.

What the hell just happened?

"We need to talk to Eli," Sofia said suddenly. "Just recently, he thought he saw Adelle cheating on him with my father."

She didn't wait for my response before rushing off, leaving me standing alone with Kiev.

His presence still gave me shudders. Even though I was aware that what I'd witnessed was an illusion, it didn't stop the urge to rip out his throat, or at least maim him a little. Despite the fact that I'd made up with him, my temper still tended to be much shorter with him than others on this island because of the past we shared. And I wasn't sure that much could ever be done about that.

"You really thought I'd do that?" he asked, staring at me.

I shot him a glance. I didn't believe that my Sofia would do that. But as for Kiev? The truth was, I didn't know. He'd made no secret of the fact that he'd held a strong attraction for her years ago. I'd even feared that he'd have his way with her while she was under his care in The Blood Keep. I didn't know how strong his attraction for her still was. Although he'd changed, he still had a dark side… like the rest of us.

An awkward silence fell between us as I chose not to answer. It didn't last long though, as Sofia came racing back through the forest, with both Aiden and a bleary-eyed Eli trailing along behind her. I was glad to see that Eli seemed to have recovered from his neck injury.

Aiden was the first to speak. "Yuri and Claudia. Landis and Ashley. Zinnia and Gavin. Do you know why they were all absent from the funeral?"

I stared at him. "Why?"

"All had arguments. I believe all about the same thing—one of them thought the other was cheating."

Aiden didn't need to say another word for my suspicions to begin to finally align and make sense.

I slammed my fist against a wooden post, cursing beneath my breath. "I knew we shouldn't have let those witches onto the island."

"Derek, but how—?" Sofia stammered.

I shook my head. I didn't know how. But now, in a rush of thoughts, I was beginning to guess why.

"We need to find Mona," I said.

I began lurching forward toward the direction of their home along the beach while the others followed me. That was the logical place to start. Perhaps the vision I'd had of her was indeed real, and she'd magicked herself back to the house, narrowly missing Kiev, who'd come out looking for her.

As we neared the stretch of beach where the vampires were housed, my heartbeat quickened. Dozens of vampires and werewolves stood out on the beach, all staring and pointing at a billowing vortex of smoke rising up from the top of Kiev's building.

"What the—" Kiev swore and, before any of us could hold him back, he hurtled into the burning building.

"He's mad!" Aiden gasped.

I couldn't argue with my father-in-law.

We waited with bated breath for Kiev to emerge. His siblings, Erik and Helina, rushed over to us. Their eyes were wide with panic.

"What happened?" Helina cried.

I shook my head, my eyes still fixed on the fiery building's entrance.

We all breathed a sigh of relief when Kiev finally

emerged from it. But our relief didn't last long as he staggered toward us empty-handed. His clothes were singed, he had burns all over his body and ash smeared his face.

He fell to his knees, wheezing.

"Mona's gone."

Chapter 31: Ben

About half an hour after my father injected me, blood began to spill from my nostrils and I felt an overwhelming urge to retch again. Drawing open the window, I coughed up mouthfuls more of it.

I didn't understand why, but one thing was becoming clear to me. My body rejected animal blood. I'd had no problem consuming Yasmine's blood.

I slammed the window shut, breathing heavily. I sensed a tinge of human blood in my room, carried in by a breeze. My mouth watered.

I paced up and down my room, trying to distract myself from the hunger tearing through my stomach. But it was impossible. It felt like every cell of my being was craving human blood.

Guilt still gripped me for what I'd done to Yasmine. And yet I realized I wouldn't hesitate to kill again if it meant satisfying my hunger. I tried to feel guilty at the realization, but I was too consumed by bloodlust. Remembrance of the taste of her blood filled my mind, tantalizing my taste buds. My mouth tingled just at the memory of it.

I walked back over to the window, staring out at the starry night sky.

I can't remain here like this.

I'd thought it would get better. I'd thought, as my parents had hoped, that I'd get accustomed to animal blood and it would fill me up enough to not be so dangerous, not be such a threat to humans. But I didn't see how that could ever happen when I couldn't even hold down the stuff for more than a few minutes.

This island was under enough stress as it was without me going around murdering people. And I didn't want to risk taking the life of another person I cared for. What would become of The Shade if they couldn't even trust their own prince?

Although it cut me to think of how it would hurt my parents, there only was one solution. And I needed to do it sooner rather than later.

Now that I'd just thrown up again, I felt hungrier than ever.

I clutched the handle of my door. It was locked. I cast my eyes around the room. Grabbing a backpack, I began piling items of clothing and personal belongings into it. I emptied my cupboard, drawers, and looked under my bed for money. While I had a few notes, it wouldn't be enough. I didn't know how long I would need to stay away.

I couldn't break down the door. It would wake my parents.

Swinging the bag onto my back, I pulled open the window. My breath hitched as I looked down—the forest ground was hundreds of feet down. I climbed out, gripping hold of the wooden frame. With one forceful swing, I hurled myself against the window ledge next to mine. It was the window in the hallway. I was relieved that it was slightly open.

Hauling myself up, I pulled the window fully open before climbing back into the apartment. I held my breath, listening for any sign of my parents stirring. The apartment was completely silent. I couldn't hear their snoring... or even breathing for that matter. I wondered if they were even in the apartment.

I padded along the carpet and headed to my father's study. Easing the door open, I walked to the safe and entered the code. I pulled out several wads of cash before closing it again. We had plenty of money on this island. More than we needed. It wouldn't be missed.

Next, I reached into the filing cabinet next to the safe and pulled out one of the several photocopies of Mona's map my father stored there. I wasn't sure why I'd taken it, but there was no harm having it.

After stuffing both the money and the map into my bag, finally I walked over to my father's desk. I picked up a pen and ripped off a piece of paper from his notepad.

I stared at the paper for several minutes before putting the pen to it.

No matter how I worded it, it would cut my parents deep. So I might as well just be as direct as possible. I didn't have much time after all. I couldn't be caught. If I was, I didn't know that I would be able to escape the island.

Bending down over the desk, I began to write:

"I can't hold in animal blood.

I've left, because it's what is best for The Shade. Our people are safer without me.

I don't know when I'll return. But, please, don't come looking for me.

Ben."

I stared at my handwriting a few more moments, jagged and messy from the way my hand was shaking. Then I slid the note into the center of the table where my father would see it.

I regretted not being able to say goodbye to everyone I cared for in The Shade. Especially Abby. We'd become close friends in recent weeks. I hoped that she'd understand.

Drawing a deep breath, I left the room. Although I guessed that it would be locked, I tried the front door. I was right to have tried. It was open. I couldn't use the elevator in case I bumped into someone. Climbing onto the balcony railing, I leapt into a nearby tree. My heart hammered in my chest as I closed the distance between myself and the ground. As soon as my feet hit the ground, I lost no time in racing forward. I whizzed through the trees so fast, I would have appeared to be but a blur to any onlooker.

Once I reached the Port, I ducked down low. I had to keep myself hidden in shadow as much as I could. I arrived at the bay of submarines and, scanning the line for the smallest one, opened the hatch and lowered myself inside.

As I seated myself in the control room and started up the engine, navigating it away from the harbor and into the open sea, I didn't know where I would go or what I would do. Or how I would survive as this beast I was still trying to understand myself.

I didn't understand why I was different from all the other vampires. They adjusted to animal blood. Their bodies didn't expel it like it was poison. They didn't feel the urge to violate the law of the island by harming humans.

I didn't know what was different about me, or what was to become of me. But whatever the case, one truth remained: I no longer belonged in The Shade.

Chapter 32: Annora

Anselm had been gracious enough to grant me the corpse of a black-haired woman without asking many questions. I'd noticed it piled up outside the royal kitchens as I was escorted back toward the gate. After the guard led me back out onto the beach and set me down next to the circular hole in the sand I'd arrived through, I looked over the body. I waited until the ogre had disappeared behind the iron gates before starting work on it. This woman looked very different from Rose. Her hair and height were the only similarities. I walked over to the ship I'd found the chest of daggers in and started running thin cuts along the body, enough so that no discernible features could be made out. Since the hair also wasn't the right length, I slashed the tips to give them a ripped effect.

Dragging the body with me toward the edge of the gate, I leapt through with it.

Once I arrived at the other end of the tunnel, I had to be careful. If Caleb or Rose found me before it was time, my plan would be spoiled. And more than just the plan lay in the balance. Anselm was scheduled to come to collect his gift soon and if Caleb got in the way, Anselm would realize I might not be who I said I was. No, I couldn't afford for that to happen.

I dragged the body closer to our tree and left it in some bushes while I crept to see if Caleb or Rose were anywhere in sight. They weren't. I circled the trees closest to ours, looking upward and straining my eyes to spot the bees' nest I had noticed the day before. On spotting it, I hurried back to fetch the body and placed it directly beneath the nest—some meters away from the foot of our own tree. Then I covered it with piles of leaves. Fortunately, the body had already been treated with preservatives by the ogres, so it would still look fresh. But there wasn't much I could do about the fact that the corpse was naked. Caleb would just have to assume that her underwear ripped away from her body during her fall to the ground, and sharp branches had sliced her skin. Since Rose seemed to like roaming around in the treetops so much, I hoped it wouldn't be too implausible a story that she might have tried to gather some honey. It was far from ideal, that was for sure. But it was the best I could do. I had to hope that the shock would leave him too devastated to think much further into it.

Then I waited until Caleb and Rose returned to their beds before approaching them. It stung me to see the way they were dressed, and the way he was touching her. And when Caleb told me he no longer loved me, I wasn't sure that I could keep up my act. But I had to, so I did. I told them what I needed to and left them alone that night, and the next morning.

It was fortunate that Caleb had decided to leave Rose in the tree while he ventured into the jungle. Otherwise I would have had to cause a distraction. Now, all I had to do was uncover the corpse, loosen the bees' nest from its branch and cover up Rose's screams as Anselm carried her away... and of course hurry to the well to say goodbye to Rose. The latter wasn't difficult. Caleb seemed so consumed in grief as he tried to brush away the bees, I doubted he even noticed me slip away.

He was still in the same spot that I'd left him in once I returned having bidden farewell to Rose. He was crouched down on the ground next to the body, his head on his knees. He was so still, I wondered if he was even breathing.

I hated how affected he was by her. I wondered if he would have ever grieved so intensely for me.

I snapped myself out of my jealousy. I needed to think straight now. Caleb and I needed to leave this island as soon as possible. It wasn't safe to be here any more. If the black witches found out about my visit to Anselm and that I'd handed Rose Novak right to them, my life wouldn't be worth living. And they were still after Caleb too for stealing away Rose from Lilith's cave.

I approached Caleb cautiously, touching his shoulder. The moment I touched him, his hand shot out and gripped my throat. Before I could even gasp, he slammed my head back against a tree trunk. Pain seared through my skull. It felt like it had cracked. He held me in place by my throat, his eyes blazing into mine.

"You did this," he snarled.

"What?" I choked, my eyes widening.

His grip on my neck tightened as he slammed me against another tree. His claws extended. I felt their tips beginning to dig into my flesh.

"C-Caleb, no! I swear!"

His eyes darkened. He seemed to be losing control.

I thrashed, trying to pry his hands away from me. "There's no way I could have done this," I wheezed. "I haven't been near our tree since morning."

"You lie."

"No!" I began to panic as his claws dug so hard into me, they drew blood. I clutched his hair. "Please, Caleb. It's me... Annora," I whispered. "Don't do this to me."

Growling in frustration, he threw me to the ground. When I looked up again, he had vanished into the jungle.

He just needs time to get over the shock. He'll be all right.

Shaking, I climbed up our tree and sat on our bunk. I waited there for hours, and by night, Caleb still hadn't returned. I began to fear that perhaps he had finished the boat and left the island without me.

No, I can't believe he would do that…

During the early hours of the morning I was seriously debating leaving and going to look for him. But I forced myself to trust that he would return. If I left, I might get lost in the jungle and wouldn't be here if he came back.

I was right to wait. Just before sunrise, he returned. I heard the snapping of twigs as he walked on the ground at the foot of our tree. He moved toward the body. I moved in the tree to better see what he was doing. He lifted it up and carried it over to the lake. I stared as he laid it down on a rock and began piling dried leaves and twigs around it. A few minutes later, there was the spark of a fire. I climbed down to the ground and walked toward him. I stopped twenty feet away, giving him space as the fire climbed higher and higher.

He knelt on the ground, staring into the flames as they licked the crisp morning air.

Dawn was beginning to break in the distance. Today would have to be the day we left. I'd felt nervous about staying the night here. But Caleb had needed the space.

I waited for an hour or so, watching as he remained

motionless in front of the fire, watching as the flames consumed the body. He remained in the same position, still watching the corpse even as it faded into a pile of ashes.

Finally he stood up and walked over to me, his eyes red, his face ashen.

I thought he was going to say something as he walked toward me, but he brushed right past me.

"Wait," I called, hurrying to keep up with him. "Where are you going?"

"Leaving," he said, his voice hoarse.

I breathed out in relief.

"Have you finished the boat?"

He ignored me.

I caught his hand and tugged on it, trying to force him to stop and look at me.

He yanked his hand away from me. "Don't touch me."

The way he was glaring at me cut me to the core. I'd hoped that he would be less likely to blame me after all the pains I'd taken in setting up Rose's kidnapping. I supposed it was foolish to expect that after I'd already admitted trying to kill Rose on the submarine.

"Caleb, please." My voice broke as I knelt at his feet. "Don't leave me alone on this island. I swear to God I didn't push Rose off that tree." He paused, turning around to stare at me. I hoped that I was getting through to him. "I know you don't love me any more. I-I can't expect you to. But please don't leave me here. Drop me off at the nearest shore, and you'll never have to see my face again."

I tried to read his expression. A myriad of emotions seemed to break through the mask he'd been assuming at once. Grief. Anger. Confusion. Conflict. I thought he was about to turn away again, but instead, gripping my shoulder, he pulled me to my feet and pulled me onto his back. And then he hurtled forward through the jungle.

It split my heart in two to think that the thought of abandoning me on a nearby shore was probably the only reason he'd agreed to my proposal. Of course, I had no intention of allowing him to do any such thing... but right now, the important thing was to just get off this island by any means necessary. I could deal with the consequences of my words later.

It wasn't long before we reached the beach and he

dropped me onto the sand. I got to my feet, staring at a small, half-completed boat.

He seemed to not even feel the sun beginning to rise in the sky as he began working furiously to finish it. He certainly hadn't lost his skill.

Tears welled in my eyes as I watched him. It brought back memories of the time when my father would moor our ship in his father's yard. I'd always find an excuse to be in the part of the ship Caleb was carrying out repairs in. And I'd often catch him glancing at me when he thought I wasn't looking.

What I wouldn't give to turn back time…

I tried to offer to hold a broad leaf over him while he worked, since the sun was beginning to sizzle his skin, but he brushed me aside.

I was stunned that within what felt like less than two hours, the boat was completed. It was a small boat constructed of a mixture of pieces from the old submarine and wood he'd felled in the jungle. He'd built a small covering over it to protect him from the sun. We didn't know if it would float yet. But there was only one way to find out.

I followed after him as he pushed the boat into the

waves and leapt inside. I gripped the edges and hauled myself up after him. I moved to the end of the boat while he raised the sails he'd constructed of tarpaulin he'd found in the wrecked submarine.

We had no engine, of course. This was an old-fashioned boat. The type Caleb had been used to sailing all those years ago. The type Caleb and I had been planning to travel the world in after we got married…

I suspected that Caleb's hope was that we would come across a larger, faster vessel we could jump aboard, which could take us to land. Because this boat would only get us so far.

I didn't know where I'd go with Caleb once I managed to get him to stick with me. But it didn't matter. As long as I was with him, I didn't care. We'd figure something out.

But I was getting ahead of myself. First things first.

After Caleb set our course and we began gliding through deeper waters, he sank down on the floor beneath the covering. He turned his back on me and buried his head in his hands.

I shifted in my spot, trying to rack my brain as to how I would even start convincing him to not take me to shore and abandon me.

I found myself just staring at him. I still wasn't used to the feelings that erupted in me whenever I laid eyes on him. Even though he seemed lost to me right now, my yearning for him was just as intense as ever. It pained me to see how sore and blistering his skin was from the sun's rays. And it was showing no signs of healing. I wondered how long it had been since he'd last drunk blood...

Blood.

The word rang through my mind like a bell.

Blood was the start of Caleb's and my downfall.

Could it also be the end of it?

I looked down at my palms. Then at the pile of unused nails lying on the deck few feet away.

I knew Caleb had a particular weakness for my blood. I also knew the consequences that would come with tricking Caleb into drinking it.

He would crave me. Desire me. Possess me.

Perhaps even consume me.

But as I looked at him across the deck, still so distant from me as he mourned the loss of Rose Novak, I realized that I'd found my answer.

There really is no other way...

CHAPTER 33: ROSE

As Anselm and I reached the exit of the tunnel, we went hurtling through the air and landed on sand. I tried to scramble away from the creature as soon as we reached the end of the tunnel and landed on a beach. Before I could even fully take in my surroundings, he grabbed my arm and, pulling out another silk handkerchief from his waistcoat, tied it around my eyes.

Still gagged, I couldn't even scream.

I felt him pick me up again and begin walking.

Where is he taking me?

There was a knocking against metal. And then the

deafening sound of heavy doors creaking open.

"Your Highness," a rasping voice said. "Would you like me to carry her for you?"

I shuddered as Anselm's rough lips brushed against my earlobe.

"No," he said, breathing heavily into my ear. "I'd rather handle this little beauty myself."

He started walking again. I kicked and thrashed, but he held me in place.

What felt like the next half hour passed with the sounds of his footsteps in my ear. At some point, the light seemed to dim and I heard the opening of a door, so I could only assume we'd gone inside. The sound of Anselm's footsteps turned from what sounded like crunching over stones to a clacking against some kind of smooth surface. I shivered. The air seemed to be getting colder by the moment as Anselm continued walking forward. I felt him climbing several flights of stairs.

Finally he stopped, and another voice spoke a few feet away from us. It sounded eerily similar to Anselm's voice, except that it was a little deeper and older-sounding.

"So this is her?"

Footsteps approached and leathery fingers brushed against my cheek.

"Yes," Anselm said. I was so close to his chest, I could feel his voice rumbling through it.

The fingers tugged on my blindfold, loosening it and pulling it down. My heart pounded as I found myself staring up at an almost splitting image of Anselm, except that he had silver streaking his hair and more lines in his face. I was granted this sight for but a moment before the creature fastened the blindfold over me again.

"Do you approve?" I could tell by Anselm's tone of voice that he was smiling.

"She needs to be fattened. Otherwise, yes."

What are these creatures?

"We shouldn't mix her in with the other girls. This one's special. I'll give her private quarters in the west wing."

"Of course."

Anselm continued walking. More stairs were climbed, more floors crossed, and by the time I felt him lowering me to the ground, my whole body was shaking. Not with terror, but rage.

I kept replaying the few seconds before Anselm had jumped with me through the gate. Annora's smug tone of voice. Her smile as she waved goodbye.

I was burning up inside.

I couldn't believe that I'd just been kidnapped again. I was beginning to lose count of the number of times it had happened in the last few months.

I swear, this is the last time I'm going to be swung over someone's shoulder like a sack of onions...

A door clicked open. I was dragged forward and pushed down onto a cold, smooth floor. The blindfold was removed again, and finally so was my gag. I coughed and spluttered, the edges of my lips stinging.

I turned around, expecting to see Anselm, but the door slammed shut again before I had a chance to swear at him. I cast my eyes around, taking in my surroundings. My breath hitched at the beauty of the room I was standing in. I hadn't expected to be brought to such a luxurious room. In the center was a dark mahogany four-poster bed covered with fur blankets. A large gold-plated mirror was fixed to the wall opposite me, and next to it was a dressing table. The floor was made of some kind of polished white stone. In the far corner was another door, left ajar. A bathroom, I assumed. Strangely, the whole room smelled of roasted spices.

My eyes were drawn to the source of light in the room. Tall window panes took up an entire wall. I gasped as I approached them. Pitch-black mountains stretched out for as far as the eye could see. Gray smoke swirled around their sharp peaks. The sky was overcast, no sign of the sun breaking the thick, low-hanging clouds.

Where am I?

"Hullo." A thick voice spoke behind me.

As I whirled around, the blood drained from my face. I stumbled back as my eyes fell on a grotesque-looking creature... an ogre. Had it not been for Brett, I wouldn't have even known what it was. But it shared the same thick, muddy brown skin, tusks, small squashed nose, and bulging eyes. There was only one real difference between this ogre's physiology and Brett's. And that was that this ogre had long hair and breasts. It—or rather, she—wore a long beige smock over her bulging form.

She plodded forward, holding out a meaty hand. I

kept my arms firmly behind my back, pressing myself harder against the wall.

"I'm Arabella… But you can call me Bella."

Bella? I would have laughed had my situation not been so dire.

"I'm to be your maid while you're in the west wing," she continued.

Although I wasn't making any motion to indicate that I was going to accept her handshake, still she held out her hand expectantly.

"Where am I?" I asked, my eyes narrowing on her.

Her expression suddenly tightened. She cast her eyes downward and dropped her hand back to her side. "His Highness didn't permit me to answer questions."

"What is Anselm? He doesn't look like you."

She chewed on her fat lower lip, shaking her head apologetically.

I exhaled in frustration. "What can you tell me?"

"Not really supposed to talk other than introduce myself," she mumbled.

I brushed past her, walking over to the bed and slumping down on the mattress. My eyes followed *Bella* as she crossed the room and opened a cupboard. She pulled out a light pink robe made of silk and handed it to me. Since I was still wearing the now battered bikini Caleb had made for me, I eagerly pulled it over myself.

Then Bella moved toward a door to my left that I hadn't noticed until now. I followed her inside. It was a kitchen. There was a stove and a deep clay oven, and the walls were lined with steel pots, knives, plates and other cutlery.

"Was expecting you about now," she said, reaching for a pan of oil on the stove and shaking it. It hissed, and gave off a strong spicy smell. She reached for a larger pot sitting on the fire behind it and lifted the lid. It was filled to the brim with a kind of colorful stew. *How many people is she cooking for here?* Tipping the oil into the stew and mixing it all together, she reached for a bowl and slopped some into it.

She nodded toward the bedroom. "Go and sit."

I hesitated. I'd lived on nothing but fruit for the last few days and I was famished. But I had no idea what it was she was about to feed me. And I didn't dare ask. I was sure the answer would make me feel queasy.

Seeing no other option, I did as Bella had requested. Since there was no other table in the room, I sat down at the dressing table. She placed the bowl in front of me and dunked a spoon in it.

Bella sat down cross-legged on the floor next to me, watching as I took my first mouthful. I was pleasantly surprised as the warm liquid glided down my throat. It was unlike anything I'd tried before, but it was tasty.

"What's in it?" I couldn't help but ask.

She flashed me a goofy grin, revealing a set of wide yellowing teeth. "It's a secret… my special recipe."

Her answer hardly made me feel more comfortable about what I was putting in my mouth, but since I wasn't retching yet, I finished the bowl.

"You want some more?"

I shook my head. My stomach had shrunk, and one bowl was more than enough. She got up and took my bowl into the kitchen. I heard water gushing and pots clanking as she began to wash up.

Now that I had some proper nourishment in me, I found myself able to think a little clearer. I pushed my chair back and walked up to the mirror. I slipped a hand beneath my gown, running it over the torn leaves covering my chest.

Caleb.

I closed my eyes, wincing. It cut me to the core to think that he'd be all alone with Annora now. I hated to think what they might be doing without me. I prayed that he was strong enough to keep resisting her and not give her a second chance.

My blood boiled as I recalled Annora's 'apology' and declaration that she would leave Caleb alone. She was full of more crap than any giant bird nest could hold.

I didn't know what horrors lay in wait for me in this ghastly realm. I didn't know what would become of me. Or how I would ever escape.

But as I stared at myself in the mirror, the fury running through my veins left no room for fear. I felt like a ball of fire.

And I did know one thing.

Annora was going to rue the day she ever messed with a Novak.

Ready for the next part of Derek, Sofia and the twins' story?

A Shade of Vampire 13: A Turn of Tides is available to order now.

Please visit www.bellaforrest.net for details!

Also, if you'd like to stay up to date about Bella's new releases, please visit: www.forrestbooks.com, enter your email and you'll be the first to know.

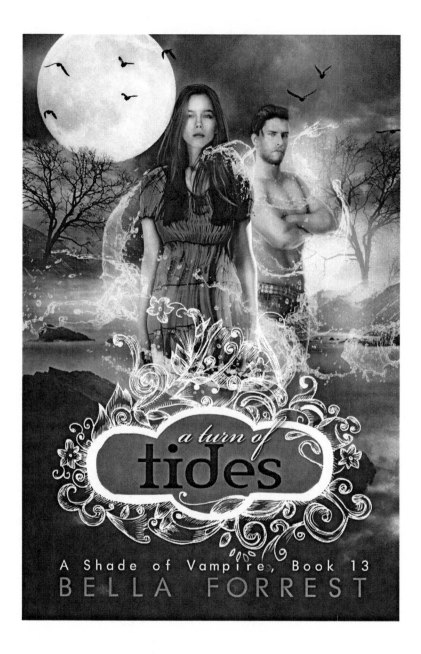

a turn of tides

A Shade of Vampire, Book 13

BELLA FORREST

A Note About Kiev

Dear Shaddict,

If you're curious about what happened to Kiev during his time away, and how he came upon Anna, I suggest you check out his completed stand-alone trilogy: *A Shade of Kiev*.

Kiev's story will also give you a deeper understanding of the Shade books and the kind of threat Derek and Sofia are now up against.

Please visit my website for more details: www.bellaforrest.net

Best wishes,
Bella

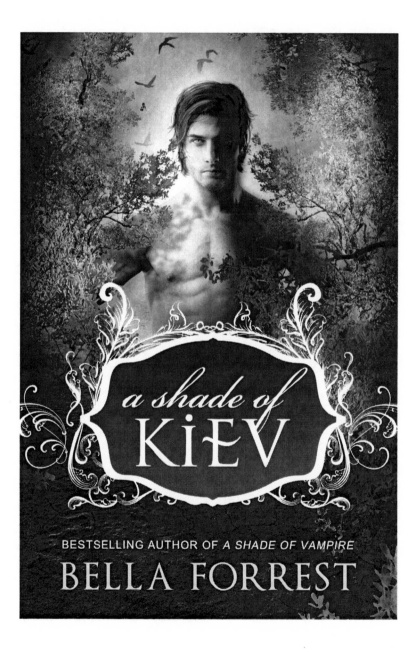

a shade of
KiEV

BESTSELLING AUTHOR OF *A SHADE OF VAMPIRE*

BELLA FORREST

a shade of
KiEV 2

BESTSELLING AUTHOR OF *A SHADE OF VAMPIRE*

BELLA FORREST

a shade of KiEV 3

BESTSELLING AUTHOR OF *A SHADE OF VAMPIRE*

BELLA FORREST

CPSIA information can be obtained at www.ICGtesting.com
Printed in the USA
LVOW11s1149100416

482958LV00006BA/696/P